the second life of linus hoppe

anne-laure bondoux

the
second
life of
linus
hoppe

LA SECONDE VIE DE LINUS HOPPE

translated from the french by

catherine temerson

DELACORTE PRESS

Published by
Delacorte Press
an imprint of
Random House Children's Books
a division of Random House, Inc.
New York

Visit us on the Web! www.randomhouse.com/kids
Educators and librarians, for a variety of teaching tools, visit us at
www.randomhouse.com/teachers

Library of Congress Cataloging-in-Publication Data

Bondoux, Anne-Laure.
[Seconde vie de Linus Hoppe. English]
The second life of Linus Hoppe / Anne-Laure Bondoux ;
translated from the French by Catherine Temerson.
p. cm.
Originally published: France: Bayard Editions Jeunesse, 2002, under title:
La seconde vie de Linus Hoppe.
Summary: Having given up his privileged life for the freedom to make his own
decisions, fourteen-year-old Linus escapes the drudgery of Realm Two and joins
with others to battle the power behind the Great Processor.
ISBN 0-385-73230-9 (trade) — ISBN 0-385-90256-5 (glb)
[1. Social classes—Fiction. 2. Interpersonal relations—Fiction. 3. Science fiction.]
I. Temerson, Catherine. II. Title.

PZ7.B63696Sec 2005
[Fic]—dc22
2004028811

The text of this book is set in 12.5-point Apollo MT.

Book design by Angela Carlino

Printed in the United States of America

October 2005

10 9 8 7 6 5 4 3 2 1

BVG

ALSO BY ANNE-LAURE BONDOUX

The Destiny of Linus Hoppe

(the companion to *The Second Life of Linus Hoppe*)

chapter 1

Linus's face was distorted with pain from hours of bending over a conveyor belt. He held back a groan as he grabbed a carton and swung it around onto another conveyor belt that led to an automatic sealer. As he turned again, a new carton appeared with its heavy load of cans and bottles. How many of these had he lifted since he'd first been put to work on this packaging assembly line? Probably hundreds, maybe thousands, all in six months.

On the day following the exam, after Linus had spent his first night in the transit home, the supervisor of the Subterranean Training Zone had informed him of his work assignment. Linus had thought it was a joke. It was too absurd that this sort of strenuous manual labor still existed. These tasks had been automated ages ago. But seeing the supervisor's hostile look now, Linus no longer felt like laughing. The conveyor belts had started back up with a deafening racket, and he had to get to work.

Other teenagers were posted all along the main conveyor belt. There were about thirty displaced examinees, and like Linus, they all had a lost, slightly panicked look in their eyes. The conveyor belt gathered speed. Linus had no time to think. Whenever he fell behind, the supervisor threatened to penalize the entire group, and the others cursed him, afraid of being punished. In a matter of days after arriving, they all had fallen into a routine. No one grumbled or complained anymore. The cartons and bottles became their sole objects of concern.

At first the monotonous motions allowed Linus's thoughts free rein. As he loaded and unloaded cartons, he recalled his former life in Realm One: his spacious house in the Protected Zone; the garden with its trees; the cloudless Sundays spent with his parents and his sister, Mieg; their vacations at his grandmother's house in Florida; the succession of blissfully quiet days . . . Heartsick with grief, Linus went over the sequence of events that had landed him in this Realm Two transit home.

It had all started several months before the exam. Like all fourteen-year-old students, Linus was preparing to go before the Great Processor. He would be admitted permanently into one of society's four realms, decided by his score. There was little doubt that he would follow in his family's footsteps and continue to live in Realm One, among the elite, for the rest of his life. The sole purpose of the exam was to validate the perfect life for which he had been programmed since birth. The problem was Linus didn't feel happy in this codified, rigid system. He found it stifling.

While surfing on the World Exchange Forum, he met a strange boy who lived in Realm Two. Though Yosh Bresco didn't live very far away—only at the other end of Paris—he might as well have been on another planet. In the Open Zone, where Yosh lived, gasoline-powered cars still polluted the air, dogs barked viciously behind apartment doors, and people smelled bad from the putrid fumes of the Industrial Zone. Linus didn't envy Yosh, yet meeting him was a good thing. The more contact he had with Yosh, the more curious Linus became about life in Realm Two. A new feeling of rebelliousness and anger led him to nurture a crazy idea: he wanted to change the course of his destiny.

The first person he confided this desire to was Chem Nogoro, his best friend. Chem was a brilliant but insolent student, doomed to end up in Realm Three. He was a computer genius, a programming geek. Thanks to him, Linus made contact with a resistance network headed by Mr. Zanz, and from then on, things had gathered steam.

Linus and Yosh were able to elude the surveillance of the electronic police and to cheat on the exam. Chem succeeded in breaking into the Great Processor's programs and switching Linus's and Yosh's scores in real time so that Linus wound up in Realm Two.

"A really smart move!" Linus said ironically to himself now. He started to laugh as the cartons piled up on the conveyor belt.

"Linus Hoppe! A ten-point penalty!" the supervisor yelled as soon as he heard him.

Linus shrugged and set to work again. One carton, two cartons . . . Each time he bent his head, his neck hurt. His throat had been swollen for several days and the skin under his chin itched constantly. On the advice of Sadko

Flavitch, the only friend he had made in the home, he'd put in a request for a medical visit. But to date no physician had shown up. So he had wrapped a scarf around his sore neck, though that didn't really bring much relief.

Looking around, Linus once again realized the magnitude of his mistake. No one had warned him about the transit home. In his mind, switching test scores had meant he'd live with a family in Realm Two and his parents would be allowed to visit him; he would live near Mr. Zanz and easily stay in contact with Chem and organize demonstrations. He had believed that adventure awaited him.

But he hadn't seen Yosh in six months, or Chem—who had been sent to Realm Three—or Mr. Zanz, or his parents, or Mieg. Instead of finding adventure, he was trapped in this warehouse with cartons, a broken back, and shattered dreams.

A shrill alarm suddenly rang out in the STZ, and the machines came to a stop. It was the end of the workday. Linus dropped the last carton onto the conveyor belt. He straightened himself slowly, hands on his hips, like an old man. His forehead was dripping with sweat, but he didn't have the energy to wipe it. With hesitant steps, he left his workstation and joined the silent line of students, all of whom were drained and exhausted after the eight hours spent in the overheated warehouse.

Linus noticed Sadko in front of the elevator door making his way toward him. With his straight blond hair and tall, thin body, Sadko resembled a scrawny giraffe. Linus sighed. Here was someone who was never supposed to see the inside of the transit home. After the exam, Sadko had expected to live with his mother again, in Realm Two. But when he left the lecture hall, a supervisor told him that he couldn't go home; his mother had died suddenly that afternoon. How had she died? Of what? Sadko still didn't know. Being an orphan, he had been sent to the home. He hadn't even been given permission to attend the funeral.

"Are you all right?" Sadko asked, glancing worriedly at Linus's throat. "Still hanging in there?"

Linus tried to smile in response, but even his facial muscles hurt.

"You can't go on like this," Sadko said. "You've got to see a doctor."

Outside, startled by the light, they blinked like blinded moles; then they quickly slipped their jackets on and pulled their hoods over their damp hair. The December air was biting cold.

Sadko led Linus into a small courtyard surrounded by the austere buildings of the transit home. For the past six months, this concrete rectangle had been their sole recreation area. They weren't allowed to leave the home or receive visits. The displaced students represented the failures of the system and, as such, were hidden away like shameful beasts. The only glorious reclassification was that of students like Yosh, who'd acquired entry into Realm One. These students were respected and pampered, and the authorities immediately found them foster families worthy of their achievement. But the others, those being upgraded from Realm Three or Realm Four, were too weird to appear in public. And Linus was looked upon as the black sheep in his group. As far as he knew, he was the only one who had lived in Realm One. His type of failure was particularly humiliating.

"Come take cover," Sadko said, looking up at the darkening sky.

The first drops fell; then a freezing rain started to pour down on the potholed courtyard, rapidly forming puddles in the hollows all along the small mound of grass and the tall, locked entrance gates. Linus brought a hand up to his burning forehead while Sadko helped him reach the door to the building. A group of exhausted, shivering students followed them in. They walked through the lobby and split into two groups, the girls on one side and the boys on the other, before climbing the stairs in silence.

In the dormitory, Linus and Sadko took off their shoes and collapsed on their beds. One by one, the other boys flopped down onto their mattresses like dead flies. They had drawn features, red eyes, ashen complexions. The only kid who seemed cut out for the STZ's grueling work rhythm was Elmer, a short, dark-haired, bad-tempered boy. Every evening he diligently updated his accounts in a notebook.

"Another twenty bonus points!" he exclaimed, rubbing his hands together. Then he turned to Linus and asked him disdainfully, "What about you? How many penalties?"

Overcome with fatigue, Linus shut his eyes and turned toward the wall without replying.

This hour before dinner was the only personal period the students were entitled to, but Linus never managed to take advantage of it. The same questions swirled in his head obsessively: Would he ever see his parents again? Would he be able to explain to them why he had wanted to change the course of his destiny? Would they understand him? Then his thoughts shifted to Mieg, Yosh, Chem, and Mr. Zanz. Where were they? What were they up to? Did they ever think of him?

He grabbed the pillow and buried his face in it, trying to silence his memories. Everyone else in the dark dormitory was half asleep. How could they rest? Try as he might, Linus just couldn't forget; it wasn't possible. Not only did he see the faces of those he loved, he relived the horrible exam. Once again he was imprisoned in the dark cubicle. He felt the steel handcuffs clamp down on his wrists and the sensors enter his mouth. Then it all flashed by: the lit screen, the violent images mixed with childhood photos, the hot and cold sensations, the stomach pain, the exploding sounds in his ears. He heard the synthetic voice asking him to state his name, then his own voice screaming, "Are you the Great Processor?" And he felt himself crashing against a wall and losing consciousness.

His nose buried in the pillow and tears welling in his eyes, he tried to catch his breath. That was what the vaunted exam, which no one ever described in detail, was like: it was torture.

Linus unobtrusively slipped his hand under the

mattress. He felt for the tiny bump under the strip of Scotch tape wedged between two metal slats.

After the exam, the organizers had distributed tablets to the examinees. They had said the tablets were "energy boosters." Linus had almost swallowed his, like everyone else had, but the dreadful vanilla smell had turned his stomach. He'd slipped the tablet into his pocket, and when he'd arrived at the transit home, he'd taken the precaution of hiding it under his mattress before his belongings were confiscated. The following day, he'd found a strip of tape in the STZ and adhered the tablet between the slats.

The more Linus thought about it, the more convinced he was that this pill had caused the collective amnesia that seemed to have struck all his fellow students after the exam. No one remembered the violence and absurdity of the test, so no one protested against the Great Processor. Unknowing families continued to send their children to the exam center.

Linus looked at his sleeping neighbor with envy and despair. Without making any noise, he stripped off the tape and held the tablet in his palm. He brought it up to his nose. By then it had lost some of its awful odor. What if he swallowed it? What if he voluntarily forgot everything? Maybe he would finally be able to sleep and accept his fate. Maybe he wouldn't feel so depressed and could start a new life. . . .

Worn out, Linus opened his mouth. He was about to put the tablet on his tongue when Sadko's voice made him start. "Are you sleeping?"

Linus clasped his hand shut over the tablet. Sadko was standing by his bed. "What's wrong, Linus? Are you crying?"

Linus wiped his eyes and threw back his blanket. "It's the fever," he said. "It makes my eyes tear."

"I forgot to tell you," Sadko mumbled, sitting down on the bed. "There's a new supervisor in the storage warehouse. Her name is Toscane."

Linus raised his eyebrows. In his present state, he had no desire to talk about girls.

"So? Is she pretty?" he asked, just to be polite.

Sadko smiled. "Not really. But she's interesting. She's the daughter of the director of the home."

Linus screwed up his eyes. The director's daughter? That didn't bode well. In this place, it was best to go unnoticed and avoid the management.

"Believe it or not, she's looking for you," Sadko said.

"What do you mean, looking for me?"

"She questioned me about you. I suppose she's curious about your coming from Realm One. You're the only such case here."

Linus felt his fever go up a notch. Though he had never breathed a word about his past to Sadko, he often had the feeling that his cheating on the exam was known to all. In fact, every once in a while, Sadko made strange innuendoes, as if he wanted Linus to confess the truth.

"What did you tell her?"

"All I told her was that you were sick and needed to see a doctor. She can put pressure on her father. She told me she had just returned from a training session in a re-education camp."

Linus sprang up, his heart skipping a beat. "You mean . . . in Realm Three?"

"Yes, of course, in Realm Three!" Sadko said. "Apparently it's awful there. I really pity those kids. Anyhow, Toscane came back to finish her training here with her father. She's supposed to take over as director of the transit home when he retires. Was it a mistake to talk to her about you?"

Linus shook his head. What if this girl had met Chem? There were probably several reeducation camps for rebels like him, but what if Toscane could give Linus news, or better yet, a message? For the first time in six months, Linus felt a glimmer of hope. He looked at Sadko and asked, "Will you point her out to me at the canteen later?"

Sadko looked doubtful. "She was supposed to eat with her father, in their on-site apartment. Anyhow, if she's looking for you, she'll come to you."

Linus sighed. Feverish and excited, he began muttering without realizing it.

"Sometimes you act weird," Sadko remarked. Then, with a knowing smile, he went back to his bed and lay down.

Linus dropped his head back onto the pillow. The vanilla-scented tablet was melting in his palm from the warmth of his skin. His hope of finally receiving news of Chem gave him the courage to wait. Slowly, he put the tablet back between the slats.

chapter 2

That night, as on every night, Linus dreamt he was opening doors. Dozens and dozens of doors with nothing on the other side, just one door leading to another. This dream wasn't a nightmare, because each time he opened a door, Linus thought it might be the last one.

The dream left him exhausted. At seven o'clock in the morning, when the lights in the ceiling fixture above his bed switched on and the other boys in the dorm started bustling about, he had trouble opening his eyes. As always, it was Elmer who finally got him out of bed, by shouting, "Step on it, please!"

Linus got up and headed to the sinks with the others. The home had very strict rules concerning the morning routine; all the dorm mates had to stay together until breakfast or no one would be served.

Linus turned on the cold water faucet and looked at himself in the mirror. His neck almost resembled a pelican's pouch. His cheeks were sunken, his jaws set, his gaze lackluster. He had dark circles under his eyes. He wondered if his parents would recognize him.

To keep from crying, Linus splashed water on his face. Before, when he had lived in Realm One, he had loved to spend time in the bathroom. The one in his parents' home had been a warm, inviting spot, adorned with green plants, and being there had calmed his nerves. He had always felt he was in a comfortable cocoon. Linus looked at himself in the mirror again. Why had he voluntarily given up that privileged life? He remembered being afraid—afraid of suffocating from an overly sheltered existence. His whole family had expected him to fit into the mold of the exemplary Realm One citizen, but that mold had seemed too big and burdensome to him. When he had compared himself to Mieg, who was so inventive, cheerful, and self-confident, he hadn't thought he'd measured up. He had longed for something else—but what?

"Hey! Step on it!" Elmer said again, pulling on Linus's pajama sleeve. "You're clean enough!"

One minute later, the boys were in the canteen. Their voices, the scraping of chairs on the tiled floor, and the tinkling of spoons in bowls reverberated off the bare walls of the room. Linus stared listlessly at the tangled swirls of vapor slowly rising from his bowl of warm milk. He wasn't hungry.

"Are you still craving one of your sister's shakes?" Sadko asked as he sat down opposite Linus. "They must have been real tasty for you to miss them so much."

Linus nodded. He missed so many things. Not just Mieg's unique shakes, which he had mentioned simply as a way of explaining his low spirits at breakfast and his incapacity to ingest anything.

"You can't recapture the past," Sadko said philosophically as he spread the yellowish contents of a plastic container on a slice of soft bread. "I'm just beginning to get used to the idea."

With a heavy heart, Linus agreed, but was unconvinced.

"You should resign yourself," Sadko continued. "What purpose does nostalgia serve? None. The dead are dead, and we have to get by without them."

The dead . . . maybe! Linus thought. *But what about the living? People who are still alive—breathing, talking, thinking? How does one erase them from one's mind? It's impossible!* Once again, he felt the cruel sting of regret: he never should have made the swap with Yosh. He should have stayed in his realm and stopped torturing himself with all those questions about society, justice, freedom, and the right to choose one's own future. Ever since he'd arrived at the home, those issues had been secondary to him.

At the entrance to the canteen, a row of supervisors was admonishing the students. "Hurry up! It's eight o'clock! Stragglers get a ten-point penalty!"

As Linus got up to hand in his tray, Sadko held him back.

"Wait! It's her! It's Toscane! Over there!" He pointed to a fat, short-haired girl who had just entered the canteen. She came straight up to them with determined steps. Linus put down his tray, his heart pounding. Toscane seemed slightly older than he, maybe fifteen or sixteen.

"You're Linus Hoppe, aren't you?" she asked him point-blank.

"Yes."

"I heard you're sick. Is that true?"

Linus raised his hand to his swollen throat and nodded.

"Follow me," Toscane ordered.

Seeing Linus hesitate, Sadko picked up Linus's tray. "Go on," he whispered. "This is your chance."

Toscane was already at the corridor leading to the home's administrative offices. Linus caught up with her. In spite of her size, she walked quickly, and her gestures conveyed nervous tension. She kept running her hand through her hair and twisting her fingers and cracking her knuckles. Linus looked at her furtively. Though her face was plump, she had delicate features, as if another Toscane lived inside this one.

"Where are we going?" Linus asked.

Toscane stopped abruptly and turned to him. Her eyes were a deep brown—so deep that they looked like tunnel entrances. Disconcerted, Linus lowered his head.

"Are you frightened?" she asked.

He shook his head.

"So come along!"

Toscane walked into a room where several supervisors were chatting and drinking coffee now that the students had left for the STZ. They turned their heads when they saw Toscane and Linus enter.

"This student is with me," Toscane called out. "Special dispensation."

Reassured, the supervisors went back to their conversations while Toscane led Linus down a second corridor. In this part of the building not one sound was audible, and the silence intensified the home's inherently disturbing atmosphere. Toscane slowed her pace, glanced over her shoulder, came to a halt, and looked Linus in the eye.

"I checked," she said in a low voice. "You're the Linus I was looking for."

Linus recoiled slightly. He wished he could avoid Toscane's penetrating gaze. "Why me?" he asked suspiciously.

"Because," Toscane said, "you can't stay here any longer. It's too dangerous."

Linus froze. Who was this girl? What was she talking about? He was on the verge of questioning her when a supervisor appeared at the end of the corridor. Toscane shuddered.

"Keep walking," she whispered. "Stay close to me and listen carefully."

Linus did as he was told. This feeling of urgency and this whiff of danger that gave him goose bumps were familiar to him. They reminded him of when he was planning his swap with Yosh. Toscane spoke in the breathless, nervous manner of someone who had something to hide.

"I came to get you out of the home," she continued, still whispering. "Don't ask me for details. The only thing important for you to know is that there's a new organization. Mr. Zanz asked me to act quickly. Do you follow what I'm saying?"

Linus was stunned and speechless. That name! She

had just mentioned Mr. Zanz. Right there, in that corridor, in that transit-home prison. It was balm to his ears, like a distant reassuring call. Toscane turned. The supervisor had just walked away, in the direction of the lobby. Toscane sighed with relief and stopped again.

"Yesterday, when I heard you were sick, I consulted your file. You requested to see a physician. I persuaded my father to agree to a medical visit, but he wants to see you before giving final permission. That's where I'm taking you—to his office. If everything goes well, it'll be very quick. The doctor is already here."

Linus ran his hand over his face. He found it difficult to understand what was happening. Six months of routine, imprisonment, despair—and now suddenly everything was moving so fast. He needed more time and more information. Unable to take another step, he stammered, "So—so you know Mr. Zanz?"

Toscane nodded. "I've known him for over a year. I'll explain later. My father doesn't know a thing, of course. And he's the suspicious type, I'm warning you. I hope your illness is visible to the naked eye."

Linus pulled down his scarf and showed her his swollen reddish neck. A smile crossed her lips. "It's nasty looking," she said. "It's perfect for our purposes. Now, be prepared to play along. If my father has the slightest doubt, he's capable of alerting the police. But we stand a good chance. I've been working on this for months, soothing my father's suspicions. Do you trust me?"

Linus pulled his scarf back up. Toscane might be lay-ing a trap for him, but something about her expression was convincing. Instinctively, he believed her. In a state of extreme agitation, he said, "I'm ready."

Toscane set off again at a brisk pace.

After going through a glass door, they found themselves in a dark, stuffy vestibule. Toscane knocked on the director's door. As she opened it, Linus experienced the sensation he had in his recurring dream.

Could this be the last door? he wondered.

chapter 3

The director's office was stark, devoid of any amenities or personal touches. But there was one object on the desk that immediately attracted Linus's attention: a computer. Probably the only one in the entire home. At the far end of the room, a frosted-glass window let in a soft light, which the director's massive frame was silhouetted against. His hands were spread out on a file.

"Come closer!" he shouted to Linus, without any preliminaries.

Linus shuddered as if he were at fault. He stepped forward, stammered a few words, then cut himself off, feeling the man's inquisitive dark eyes upon him. The same eyes Toscane had, minus the mischief. Though he was seated, the man seemed tall. His pale face was shiny from perspiration.

"Downgraded examinees from Realm One, like you, are very rare here," he began. "How do you explain your score when your whole family is so brilliant?"

Linus felt a dry, burning sensation in his throat. Since he made no reply, the director opened the file and went on. "Your father, Mr. Tobias Hoppe, is an important official in the Economic Observatory. Your mother, Francesca

Hoppe, is an expert engineer specialized in video surveillance systems. Your sister, Mieg, scored one hundred eighty-five. She's an outstanding student at the Higher Institute of Architecture." Then he added sarcastically, "You know the story of the ugly duckling, don't you?"

Linus stiffened, wounded by the director's remark. He felt Toscane's tense presence behind him. He reminded himself to play along.

"You have nothing to say for yourself?" the director shouted. "Very well! I can understand your humiliation. But be forewarned, I loathe fakers and loafers. What's your problem exactly?"

Linus made a tremendous effort to control himself. "It's my neck. It's very painful," he said, his voice breaking.

"Show me."

With trembling fingers, Linus untied his scarf. To his great surprise, the director got up, walked around the desk, and stood in front of him. Up close, his face looked even paler, almost transparent. Suddenly he bent down and roughly pressed Linus's swollen throat with his finger. Linus cried out in pain.

"Oh, a delicate creature, eh?" The man sniggered.

Linus gasped for breath. The director's shiny face danced in front of him, and the window in the background turned into a blurry splotch.

Without moving, Toscane intervened. "I wouldn't have disturbed you," she said, "if this student hadn't seemed very sick."

The director straightened with difficulty, sighed, and fell silent.

"We can't let him remain in this condition," Toscane went on. "Let me remind you of some past incidents. You just barely avoided having serious problems. I wouldn't want that to happen again."

The director went back to his desk, plopped down into his armchair, and knitted his brow. A tense atmosphere hung in the room. Linus didn't dare move a single muscle. He concentrated on trying to catch his breath and balance. Toscane didn't move either, virtually standing at attention. The director cleared his throat.

"You want to prove yourself, is that it?" he asked his daughter.

"Under the circumstances, I think it's necessary," Toscane asserted. "Allow me to supervise the visit with Dr. Ambrose and follow this student's case to his recovery."

The director drummed his fingers on the desk nervously. His face became strained with doubt and indecision.

"If we don't get medical advice, this boy could die on us," Toscane insisted. "And you know as well as I do that this could have an impact on the home's reputation . . . especially since his family is so well connected."

The director mopped his brow and shook his head, exasperated.

"All right," he said. "Go up for a medical visit immediately. As soon as it's over, I want to see Dr. Ambrose's report."

Toscane and Linus promptly left the office. Once in the vestibule, Linus filled his lungs with air, as if surfacing after being underwater too long. His heart was in his throat, pounding painfully. He had never felt so ill in his life.

"You have to hang in there, Linus," whispered Toscane, shaking him by the shoulders. "Come on! Get a grip! It's almost over now!"

She took him by the arm and led him through the corridor again, to a door that she opened with a magnetic key.

"When we get up there, do exactly what I tell you," Toscane said. "Dr. Ambrose is in on our scheme."

On the other side of the door was a badly lit landing. Everything was silent. Toscane pushed Linus toward the steps leading up to the mezzanine. She used her key again and they entered a carpeted room with paintings on the walls. Linus stopped at the threshold. This had to be the director's apartment. It was flooded with daylight. Tall transparent windows looked out on a tangle of trees with bare branches that crisscrossed against the white autumn sky. These picture windows were the only ones on that side of the building. Linus was so dazzled by the sight that he almost forgot his reason for being there. He walked toward the windows, his hands outstretched, drawn by the unhoped-for view of the outside world.

"Here's Dr. Ambrose," Toscane said behind him.

Slowly, Linus turned and saw a tall youngish woman looking at him with a serious expression. Her oval face was offset by short hair of indeterminate color, a mix of white and light brown.

"If you don't mind, I'm going to examine you," Dr. Ambrose said.

Linus nodded, snapping back to reality. He untied his scarf and went up to her. This time, he felt a hand that had a light, professional touch, instead of a brutal finger pressing down on his neck. He let himself be examined while watching Toscane out of the corner of his eye. Nervous as ever, she was pacing up and down the living room, twisting a lock of hair around her fingers.

"I'd like to check you out more thoroughly," Dr. Ambrose finally said. "Come sit down."

She guided Linus toward a sofa at the other end of the room. He couldn't help being on the verge of tears. The uncommon gentleness with which this woman treated him, the daylight, the trees, the setting—everything moved him so deeply that he felt he might break down and cry. While Dr. Ambrose opened a small metal valise, Toscane came and stood behind the sofa. She leaned down toward Linus and whispered, "We can speak freely in front of Dr. Ambrose, but mind what you say. My father is watching us."

Linus wiped his moist palms on his trousers. No need to be very clever to figure out that there were cameras and mikes in the room. At the other end of the building, locked in his small office, the director of the home was surely following the scene on his computer screen.

"You were in a Realm Three camp?" he asked Toscane.

"Let's not talk about that right now," she muttered. "The urgent thing is organizing your escape."

Linus bit his lips. The physician had just lifted his sweater and placed a cold stethoscope on his back. The instrument was directly connected to her suitcase, which transmitted the data to a microcomputer.

"But over there . . . in Realm Three, you might have seen one of my friends," Linus insisted. "Chem Nogoro."

Toscane moved away from the sofa without answering and started pacing around the room again.

"Cough a little," Dr. Ambrose requested in an exaggeratedly loud voice.

Linus complied, though it made his throat burn painfully. During his coughing fit, Toscane came closer to him and waited for it to subside.

"You did well to get sick," she whispered. "It simplifies matters. If my father agrees to release you, you'll go to the hiding place Mr. Zanz found for you."

"Why only now? What took so long?"

"Time was required to set up the new organization. It's operational again, but things are more complicated than they used to be. Things have changed over the last six months, Linus. The police have become more and more suspicious. There have been arrests. On the day of the exam, as a matter of fact."

Linus tried to absorb all these facts into his muddled mind, but felt overwhelmed. Dr. Ambrose put her electronic stethoscope away and asked him to turn toward her and open his mouth. She used tweezers to put some nanobiosensors on his swollen tonsils.

"We had planned to contact you after your release from the transit home," she whispered, bending down to examine his throat. "In previous years, the stay here lasted only two or three months; then the displaced students were sent to foster families. That's where we would have found you. But now, transit time has been extended until further notice. You must get out."

Linus glanced at Toscane. The biosensors didn't prevent him from speaking, but he had to keep his mouth open. "Ow id you eet Zanz?"

Toscane lowered her head. "A few years ago I was anorexic." She paused to tuck a stray lock of hair behind her ear. "The year of my exam, I was so weak that my father had to call a doctor. He hates letting strangers inside the home, but he had no choice. I almost died and he's still mad at himself for it." A tremulous laugh escaped from her throat. "Now it's a terrific blackmailing ploy! Did you notice before? As soon as I remind him of that episode, he feels guilty. The doctor turned out to be Dr. Ambrose. She introduced me to Mr. Zanz's network. It's no exaggeration to say she saved my life. I was finally able to imagine an alternative to spending the rest of my life here. After my exam, I started working for the organization. I did everything to reassure my father. I acted like the model child and put on weight. Too much weight, in fact."

Linus began to understand Toscane's motivations.

Living here forever would make anyone depressed. Dr. Ambrose removed the biosensors and Linus started to cough again.

"We're done!" the physician said in a forced voice. "The infection could spread. You'll need surgery, an emergency operation. I'll have to refer the matter to the director of the home immediately."

Linus stared wide-eyed at her. An operation, for him? He had never been sick, let alone inside a hospital. He touched his throat apprehensively. All at once this prospect took him back several months, to the time when he noted with bitterness that his life hadn't been marred by the slightest incident. Those days were certainly over.

"What's going to happen after the operation?" he asked, tormented with anxiety.

Dr. Ambrose leaned down to close her suitcase. "We'll explain later," she whispered. "But you should know that you will not be returning to the home. Be ready by this evening."

chapter 4

Around five o'clock, Linus heard the other boys shuf-
fling up the stairs to the second floor. They were returning from the STZ. In a minute, they would be storming
into the dorm and besieging him with questions. Linus
bent down, raised the mattress, ripped off the strip of
tape that was securing the vanilla-scented tablet, and
hastily stuffed the tablet into his pocket. The footfalls
were getting closer. Feeling oppressed, he hurriedly
folded his belongings and closed the rough canvas bag
lent by the home. Then he crossed his hands behind his
back and waited.

"Hey . . . what are you up to?" Elmer asked, surprised. He was the first to enter the dorm.

Linus was standing in front of his bed, wearing a wa-
terproof jacket that had the insignia of the home on it.
Elmer looked him over suspiciously with a nasty smirk.

"I hear you're sucking up to the director's daughter.
Did she get you excused from work today?"

One by one, the other boys came in and stopped by
his bunk. Sadko was the last to arrive, and he jostled the
others to get to Linus.

"How do you feel?" he asked, pointing to his neck. "Did you see a doctor?"

"Yes, this morning."

"So?"

"They're sending me to the hospital. I need an operation."

"Really!" Elmer exclaimed, rolling his eyes. "An operation? What next? How about a rest cure in the Bahamas?"

Sadko whipped around and stared at the small dark-haired boy. "Shut up, Elmer! Linus is sick. You can see that, can't you?"

Three other boys dragged themselves to their beds sluggishly, glancing with hostility at Linus as they went by.

"We're sick too!" one of them grumbled.

"Yeah, we're sick too!" Elmer cried out, his face distorted with jealousy. "But we're not wimps! Whereas Mr. Hoppe comes from Realm One, remember? He's lived a cushy life for fourteen years, so it's hard for him to put up with *real* life!"

The others started sniggering foolishly while Elmer went up to Linus and stood in front of him.

"What kills me," he said, "is that the director is letting you out. Even here, guys like you have privileges. It's disgusting." To demonstrate his disgust, Elmer pinched Linus's neck. Sadko didn't have time to intervene; Linus had already grabbed Elmer's arm and was twisting it sharply.

"Go ahead! Hurt me!" Elmer said, trying to repress a pained moan.

"Stop, Linus," Sadko whispered. "If you do something stupid, they won't allow you to go out."

Linus heaved a sigh and released Elmer's arm. He felt so tense, so jumpy, he had trouble controlling himself. But Sadko was right. He definitely shouldn't react to Elmer's taunts.

"What's that around your wrist?" Sadko asked as he got closer.

Linus lowered his eyes. He wished it hadn't been seen, but it was too late. When the director had given him permission to go out, he'd fastened a flat metal object with a flashing diode around Linus's wrist.

"It's a tracking bracelet," Linus admitted. "Required when you're away from the home."

Elmer, who had taken refuge on his bed, burst out laughing. "So now you look like a dog! Bowwow!"

Sadko frowned and shook his head, silently begging Linus not to pay attention to Elmer's sarcasm.

"He's right." Linus smiled. "This bracelet is worse than a leash. The director can keep track of my every move on his computer. I can't go anywhere without his knowing about it."

Sadko shrugged. "It doesn't matter. You're not going far. As soon as you've recovered, you'll be back."

"Of course," Linus mumbled.

Elmer was moving restlessly on his bed. He had opened his notebook to update his accounts.

"The hospital," he said with a pensive air. "That's not going to be free. Do you realize how many penalties that's going to cost you?"

Linus sighed. Penalties, penalties. Elmer was obsessed with penalties. Count on him to know how many. One misstep: penalty. One loud word: penalty. So, of course, a hospitalization . . .

"I don't give a hoot about penalties," Linus retorted.

"He doesn't give a hoot!" Elmer jeered.

Then he leapt out of bed, brandishing his notebook. "You won't be so stuck-up when you leave the home flat broke," he shouted. "Are you so thick that you don't understand their system, or are you putting on an act? When we get out of here, we'll all be sent to foster families, but we won't all be equal. What do you guys think? That thousands of people are going to clamor to take us in?"

All the other boys were focused on Elmer. Encouraged by his attentive audience, he explained, "Coming out of the home, each one of us will receive a cash bonus established ahead of time. But the amount shrinks with each penalty. So the more penalties, the less money. Get it?"

The boys nodded.

"And the less money you have, the less attractive you are," Elmer went on. "That's logical! Therefore the kids who have nothing will end up in the most rotten Realm Two families."

A silence fell over the dorm. Then Sadko spoke up. "What are you talking about, Elmer? What do you mean by 'rotten'? That's ridiculous. A family is a family."

"Rotten families exist," Elmer replied calmly. "I know what I'm saying. Mine was rotten. I left it in Realm Four, if you must know. And good riddance."

Linus gave a start. Elmer had lived in Realm Four. That must be why he had never spoken about his past. Realm Four: madmen, mental cases, the incorrigible . . . Elmer was ashamed of his family, ashamed of his origins. All of a sudden, Linus understood Elmer's bitterness and determination to find a way out.

"Don't ask me anything more," Elmer added. "You handle your bonus and penalty points on your own. All I know is I'm leaving the home with my pockets full of cash. That's all I'm interested in."

Linus looked at his dorm mates. Their exhausted faces, their bruised arms, their loneliness . . . He took a few steps toward Elmer.

"I sincerely hope you'll find a good family to take you in," Linus said to him. Then he seized his bag and got ready to join Toscane and Dr. Ambrose, who were waiting for him in the administrative area. As he crossed the doorway of the dormitory, Sadko rushed up behind him.

"Wait! I'll walk part of the way with you!"

They walked down the corridor, side by side, without speaking. Linus felt dazed, like a boxer who had taken a beating. He wished he could tell Sadko everything, but he knew he couldn't. Mr. Zanz and Toscane's plan depended on complete secrecy.

"Thank you for your help," he said as they reached the other end of the corridor. "Without you—"

Sadko shook his head and interrupted him. "I didn't do anything," he said.

"You did a lot. Without you, I'd have felt very lonely."

Sadko's face lit up with a smile. "All I did was guess some of your secrets. You didn't forget anything under your mattress, I hope."

Linus opened his eyes wide and dropped his bag on the floor. Sadko quickly put a finger up to his lips and added, "Calm down! I won't say anything. I'm used to not talking. My mother had secrets too."

"Your mother?"

Sadko nodded, his thin body twisting slowly from right to left to make sure no one was hanging around the corridor. Then he explained, "She was part of a group. You know what I'm talking about, don't you? A group that wasn't quite legal. She used to say that the exam and the separation into realms were unfair."

Astounded, Linus nodded to make it clear that he understood. Sadko went on in a low voice. "She had really dangerous ideas. Proof is she's dead."

"Do you . . . Do you think she died because of her involvement with that group?" Linus asked.

"I can't be sure. But she took far too many risks. Maybe she was doing the right thing, but she left me all alone, and I resent her for that." Sadko's voice cracked. His eyes tearing up, he held out his hand to Linus. "I'll stick it out until the end of the training. I'd like to find peace and quiet again, and live a normal life. You understand? But you . . . be careful. If I don't see you again, I hope it will be for the right reasons."

"That I promise," whispered Linus, overcome with emotion.

Sadko wiped his eyes and, containing his anger, added, "It's a pity to die when you have a family." Then he ran off toward the dorm.

Left by himself in the deserted, silent corridor, Linus put his hand on his chest to calm his palpitations. Sadko knew what was going on. He knew about the vanilla tablet and he probably knew that Linus had cheated on the exam. Had his mother belonged to Mr. Zanz's organization? Linus wished he could catch up with Sadko and ask him. But time was running out. His exit permit was only valid until six o'clock.

Disoriented and sad, Linus picked up his bag again. He headed toward the administrative area, vowing to do everything he could to see Sadko again one day.

chapter 5

"Everything's set up. Let's go," Toscane whispered, stuffing the official papers signed by her father into her pocket.

Linus followed her down the corridors, along with Dr. Ambrose. Their steps resonated; he checked his desire to run. To see the city again—the sidewalks, people in the street, trams, stores! To breathe again! To walk around freely! He was so excited that he bit his cheek to keep from barking like a puppy about to be taken for a walk.

When they reached the exit, Toscane put her hand on the digital decoder, then slipped her magnetic pass into the slot to open the security door. *It's all so simple when you're on the right side!* Linus thought.

Then suddenly he was out. Outside! Outside the home for the first time after six months of detention, pain, and despair. He was trembling from head to toe.

It was night. In these mid-December days, the temperature had dropped. He turned up his jacket collar and let himself be guided toward an ambulance parked in front of the metal gate.

"Let's hurry," the doctor said, opening the back door.

Linus didn't have time to see the ambulance driver's face. Toscane and Dr. Ambrose sat down on the wall seats and pushed him against the intensive care machines. The ambulance set off immediately, noiselessly, with no flashing light, like a dark vessel cutting through the night.

"Which hospital are we going to?" Linus asked after a long silence.

Instead of replying, Dr. Ambrose gently seized his wrist. Between her fingers she had a small notched key, which she inserted into the tracking bracelet. Linus watched her, incredulous. Suddenly the bracelet was unfastened and the diode went out. The "informer" dropped into Dr. Ambrose's hand.

The doctor smiled. "Now you're free, Linus," she said. She slipped the bracelet around her own wrist and locked it with the key. "I'll go to the hospital," she went on. "I'll serve as a decoy. The director will follow my movements and think he's watching you."

Linus rubbed his wrist, perplexed. "I don't understand. Don't I have to be operated on?"

"No."

The doctor heaved a sigh and explained. "You're not really sick, Linus. You're having a psychosomatic reaction. Your throat will be back to normal very soon. The only effective treatment is to set you free."

"A psychosomatic reaction?" Linus repeated, puzzled. He reached for the scarf around his neck and collected his thoughts. He knew that the body could fall ill for psychological reasons, but why swollen glands? All of a sudden, he smiled. He had just made the connection. "Chem!" he said out loud. "I've thought about him so much that . . ."

His voice choked with emotion. When Chem was five, he had been in a serious accident: a fire had destroyed his family's apartment, and he had just barely survived, with a third-degree burn on his throat. Afterward, his parents were tried by the Higher Court. They were held responsible for the fire, and the court ruling couldn't be appealed; they were prohibited from having another child. Chem didn't like to talk about it. He was so self-conscious about his scars that he always wore a scarf, even in the summer heat.

To his amazement, Linus realized he had subconsciously started to imitate his friend as a way of maintaining a link with him. He turned to Toscane eagerly.

"Think again, please. Doesn't the name Chem Nogoro ring a bell?"

"Let's not waste time on secondary issues," Dr. Ambrose broke in with annoyance. "The organization's hiding place is located along the route; we'll be there in a minute. In four days, the director will start to worry; meanwhile, Toscane will keep up the fiction for us. Her father is sure to catch on to the betrayal, but Toscane is ready; she'll join us before things get bad for her."

The ambulance wove through deserted streets and boulevards. The streetlights filed by the windows. Linus looked at them pensively. He promised himself that he would do everything he could to save Chem if he succeeded in escaping the director's surveillance and becoming free again.

Toscane chuckled with satisfaction. "In four days my father will finally understand that I'm not the person he thinks I am," she said. "I'm not like him. I'll never be like him!"

She locked her hands together, extended her arms forward, stretched like a cat, and cracked her knuckles. Glass flasks were clinking in their boxes. Leaning his forehead against the windowpane, Linus tried to sort out the questions swirling in his head. So many things had yet to be explained. His heart started to race. He had just realized something. "If I don't go back to the home," he said, "I'll be considered a deserter."

Toscane nodded, looking slightly embarrassed.

"I don't understand," Linus said. "I'll be wanted, put on file and actively pursued by the police?"

Toscane nodded again. Anguished, Linus addressed Dr. Ambrose. "But then I'll spend my life in hiding, won't I? That's not what I had in mind! Not at all! I—I just wanted to live in Realm Two. I . . ." He trailed off and bit his lip. He felt like a trapped rat. Everything had happened so fast he'd had no time to think about the consequences of an escape. In fact, he hadn't even been given a choice.

"You didn't warn me!" he wailed. "You said I was free, but that's not true. It's a lie! Even without the tracking bracelet, I . . ." He coughed, holding his throat with both hands.

Toscane shrunk in her seat. Dr. Ambrose put a hand on Linus's back. "Nothing went as planned," she said gently. "We told you, the Internet police arrested members of the old organization. That was on the day of the exam. Since then, surveillance has intensified on every level. We think the police are investigating displaced students. That would explain the extended period of time in transit homes. If you had stayed in the home, the police would have come to question you, and we had no way of protecting you there."

Linus was crushed. He recalled what Sadko had told him about his mother—the illicit group, the danger, her death on the day of the exam. Was there any correlation? "What happened exactly?" he asked through clenched teeth.

Toscane tried to calm him by putting her hand on his, but Linus waved her away roughly. She seemed to make an effort not to get annoyed. "You probably recall that Mr. Zanz ordered that everything be deleted—all servers, coded Web sites, every form of Internet evidence," she began.

Linus nodded. He had witnessed the shutting down of the entire organization several days before the exam.

"The trouble is," Toscane continued, "one group in the organization didn't obey Mr. Zanz's order. About ten people. They were sure they could continue their activities. The police tracked them down. In the afternoon, on the day of the exam, they were arrested at their homes, one by one."

Linus shut his eyes. "Was Sadko Flavitch's mother part of that group?"

"Yes."

"How did she die?"

"She was eliminated by the police squad, like the others."

Dr. Ambrose sighed. "That was the first time something like that had happened. They must have realized that the organization was growing, and wanted to show us who was strongest. Now we've had to adopt very strict measures: no more communication by Internet, telephone, or messages. Information has to be relayed in person. That's why it took us so long to find you."

Linus felt a shiver run down his spine. Dr. Ambrose looked at him sympathetically. "Some people might have talked before they were killed," she said. "Mr. Zanz was afraid the authorities would work their way back to you."

"Trust us," Toscane pleaded. "This escape was the only solution for you—and for all of us."

The ambulance slowed and drove alongside a building complex. Dr. Ambrose looked out the window. "We've arrived," she announced.

Linus sat up. If he stepped out of the ambulance, he would become a deserter, and his entire future would be jeopardized. He still had one alternative: he could ask to return to the home and wait to be assigned to a foster family. But how long would that take? And what if Toscane was right? What if the police could prove he had cheated on the exam? And what if they realized that Yosh didn't belong in Realm One? And what if they discovered that Chem was the mastermind behind the switch? Linus suddenly felt the crushing weight of responsibility. One false step and he put the lives of his friends in jeopardy.

The ambulance came to a halt.

"Come with me," Toscane said insistently. "There are people waiting for you in the hiding place."

Linus was puzzled. "What people?" he asked.

chapter 6

"Who's there?"

Groggy and numb, Linus had followed Toscane through the dark basement of one of the buildings. Now he heard footsteps and breathing to his left. The darkness was punctured by two flames from lighters.

"Who's there?" Linus repeated, his heart beating fast.

"It's me!" whispered a voice.

"And me!"

The twin flames flickered in the draft. Linus stepped back instinctively. Suddenly two smiling faces appeared before him.

"Mieg!" Linus said. "Mieg and Yosh!"

Before he realized he wasn't hallucinating, he felt his sister's arms around him. Mieg! She was there, in the flesh. Then Yosh came up and tapped him awkwardly on the back several times.

"You're alive!" Mieg cried.

"Kind of. . . ."

Linus sank into his sister's arms, burying his face in her sweater.

Toscane stood slightly apart, letting them savor the moment. Then she turned on her flashlight and opened a door adjacent to the boiler room. "Don't stay there," she whispered. "Come here!"

Clinging to Mieg, Linus went in. His legs felt shaky. Once in the light, Mieg clasped her hands around his face and took a close look at him. She was almost in tears.

"You've grown taller," she said. "And you've lost weight. And . . . you look like you have a sore throat. No question, it's time for my shake regimen again!"

That was too much. Linus burst out crying uncontrollably, laughing and hiccuping between sobs. His gaze went from Mieg to Yosh, and from Yosh to Mieg. He'd never thought so much happiness was possible.

"I've been trying for months to find out how you were," Mieg said. "Your whereabouts were unknown. Then, two hours ago, someone from the organization came to see Yosh on behalf of Mr. Zanz. He set up this meeting." She hugged Linus again. "How are you?"

Linus brushed away his tears. "Better now." He sighed. "Much better." He turned to Toscane and smiled. "You were right to insist that I follow you. Thank you, Toscane."

All four sat down at a table in the center of the room. The place was cramped; it had a low ceiling and no windows. Nevertheless, Linus felt comfortable there. It was like being in a deep underground burrow, far from all the threatening dangers above.

For several minutes, everyone was speechless. They exchanged looks; they touched one another's hands; they giggled lightheartedly. Linus looked at Yosh. He had changed. He seemed more robust and more confident than before. That might have been because of the outfit he was wearing. On the other hand, he still had the same weird hairstyle, with spiky tufts sticking out on top of his flat head like wild weeds. As for Mieg, she was as pretty as ever, though at times a shadow flitted across her eyes like a passing cloud.

"How are Mom and Dad?" Linus asked anxiously after a pause.

Mieg stroked the surface of the table. She tried to smile, but it was clear that her heart wasn't in it. "You gave them quite a shock, Linus. On the evening of the exam, we waited for you outside the exam center, on the esplanade. They kept looking for you, expecting you to appear. You can't imagine how painful it was. Groups of kids accepted into Realm One kept coming out and you weren't among them. When Mom and Dad were told your score, they were stunned. Struck dumb, like statues of salt."

Linus's face twitched. He could imagine the scene perfectly. To learn that he had caused his parents such grief was wrenching.

"In the end Dad became resigned," Mieg continued, still stroking the table. "I think he was humiliated and angry at you deep down. He assaulted us with lectures on the reliability of the exam and the Great Processor's complete impartiality. I think he was mostly trying to convince himself. As for Mom . . ." Mieg glanced at Yosh, who lowered his head. His chin was trembling. "Mom became seriously depressed. She couldn't come to terms with your absence. These past months, she's been crying and sleeping a lot. She can't concentrate on anything—not even her work. At first she and Dad argued about you constantly; now they avoid talking about you altogether. Things aren't exactly terrific."

Linus put his hand on his throat. It hurt terribly. "I never should have done what I did," he said in a pained voice. "I ended up in a transit home, working like a slave on a packaging assembly line. And I'd still be there if Toscane and Mr. Zanz hadn't tracked me down. Changing realms was a big mistake."

At those words, Yosh's whole body started to tremble. His face became flushed and he cried out, "Don't say that! If you hadn't made the swap with me, I wouldn't be in Realm One, and . . ." He couldn't go on. He leapt to his feet and started pacing up and down the room frantically, swinging his arms around like a windmill.

"No, Yosh! For pity's sake!" Mieg shouted, rushing up to him. "Please don't have a fit now! Get a grip on yourself!"

Shaken by uncontrollable tics, Yosh continued. "I wouldn't be . . . in Realm One and . . . my life would be . . . wrecked! Even if you . . . have regrets, Li . . . nus, I'm deeply thankful!"

Linus followed Yosh's movements with sorrow. "Think of your whip!" he shouted. "Do you remember?

You told me you were a lion tamer! You told me your anger was a wild beast! Crack your whip!"

Yosh's face gradually began to relax. He calmed down and Mieg led him to his chair. Once seated, he pressed his forehead against the table and took deep breaths. Toscane, amazed by the violence of the scene, said nothing and looked at the three of them in disbelief.

"Don't worry," Linus whispered to her. "When he has strong emotions, Yosh throws temper tantrums. They hit him without warning; he's been like this since childhood, but he manages to control himself."

"I'm sorry," Yosh said softly. "It makes me unhappy to know you're unhappy, Linus."

Now Linus took a deep breath. He remembered the day when they had made their pact, in front of Yosh's building. They had been so convinced that they were making the right decision. Yosh had even confessed to Linus his real reason for wanting to be admitted into Realm One. It wasn't just that he hoped to enjoy better living conditions; he had also discovered an incredible secret. He had a younger brother who had been adopted shortly after his birth by a family in Realm One. Yosh wanted to find his brother. By agreeing to swap scores with him, Linus was giving him a big opportunity: the chance to recreate a family in Realm One and envision a better future.

"Did you find him?" Linus asked, bending close to Yosh.

Yosh lifted his strange moonlike reddish face. Unable to speak, he shook his head.

"You know, I'm not really unhappy," Linus said, to console him. "I'm just . . . incredibly tired. We swapped and there's no going back on it. What bothers me is my parents."

Toscane banged the table with her fist. "You have no reason to blame yourself," she said. "You made your choice. It's your life to live, not your parents'!"

Linus looked at her, opened his mouth to reply, then changed his mind. What was there to say about something so obvious? Still, when he thought about his father's disappointment and his mother's sadness, he felt totally guilty.

"I'm going to disappoint my father too," Toscane went on. "Four days from now. Though I realize it's probably a little different. My father never loved me. When there's no affection between two people, things are much simpler."

Toscane seemed impassive, but Linus saw agitation in her dark eyes. Being the daughter of the transit home director, of that suspicious man walled up in his impersonal office, couldn't be easy. Linus wanted to ask Toscane about her mother's whereabouts, but decided to put off such questions for the time being. There was a long silence, disrupted by the rattling pipes in the adjacent boiler room.

"What about Mr. Zanz?" Mieg asked. "Wasn't he supposed to join us?"

"He's probably at the hospital with Dr. Ambrose," Toscane explained. "He has to make sure everything goes according to plan."

Linus got up from his chair and started walking around the small room. Four walls, a mattress in the corner, a table, chairs, and a bare lightbulb hanging from the ceiling. The setting wasn't exactly cheerful.

"How long am I staying here?" he asked.

"A few days," Toscane replied. "But you won't be by yourself. We're going to take turns keeping you company."

"And then what? I presume I won't be staying in a basement all my life." He kicked the mattress gently. To think that he had hoped to see the daylight and to walk freely outside . . .

"I'm sure Mr. Zanz has worked something out," Mieg reassured him. "He never does anything rashly."

Linus sat down next to her. "I can't stop thinking about Chem." He sighed. "I don't suppose you have any news from him either?"

His sister shook her head of brown curls, looking sorry.

"We were too naïve, weren't we?" Linus said. "We thought we would be able to stay in contact; we thought if we were friends, the walls between the realms would vanish."

Yosh, who had regained his composure, grabbed Linus's arm. "I'm sure it's possible," he said. "It's a question of time. Where I work . . ." He trailed off and turned to Mieg for encouragement.

"Yosh was accepted as an intern at the Administration of Persons," Mieg explained. "Can you imagine? Not bad for a pathetic Realm Two student!"

Linus opened his eyes wide. He had trouble imagining Yosh, with his weird appearance and horrendous spelling, on the staff of such a rigid institution. The Administration of Persons was the center for all the digital information recorded on ID cards, computers, and electronic mail. Yosh had made a good choice. With that job, he had every chance of tracking down his brother.

Yosh smiled and puffed out his chest. "They're completely fooled! My supervisor is very pleased with me. He's given me quite a lot of responsibility." Then he added in a confidential tone, "Their databases are filled with information. If I can succeed in decoding them, I'm practically sure I'll locate Chem one of these days."

Linus nodded, turning to Toscane. Even if she hadn't seen Chem, she could at least tell him what the reeducation camps were like. But just as he was about to ask her, Toscane shied away. She got up and walked to the door of the room, frowning.

"Did you hear something?" Linus asked, alarmed.

Toscane signaled for him not to speak and pressed her ear against the metal panel. A moment later, her mind apparently at ease, she sat down again.

"I wish Mr. Zanz would come," she said. "It's strange that he's taking so long."

Mieg glanced at her watch. "It's starting to get late. I hope Mom and Dad aren't getting worried."

Linus looked at his sister. Very soon she would be going home; she would be seeing their parents, eating dinner with them, and resuming her normal life. How he wished he could do the same. He lowered his eyes and dug his hand into his pocket without thinking. He felt the vanilla tablet between his fingers. The reunion had been so emotional, he had forgotten to mention it.

"There's something important I have to know," he said. "Please be completely truthful: do any of you remember the exam? Do you specifically remember going before the Great Processor?"

Yosh and Toscane hesitated. Mieg opened her mouth, but just as she was about to reply, the door to the room burst open. Mr. Zanz appeared, pale and panting for breath, his hair disheveled.

"Quick!" he shouted. "We have to get out of here! It isn't safe anymore!"

chapter 7

Yosh, Mieg, Toscane, and Linus sprang from their chairs
in a panic.

"I've just come from the hospital," Mr. Zanz continued. "The police arrested Dr. Ambrose. They're going to retrace the route of the ambulance and begin a search. If you stay here, they'll find you!"

Linus felt his stomach tighten. He caught Mieg by the hand. While Toscane grabbed his canvas bag, Linus drew his sister behind Yosh and Mr. Zanz, both of whom had started to run across the basement. Their steps echoed on the concrete floor. The beam from Mr. Zanz's flashlight lit up the darkness ahead of them. Toscane had trouble keeping up with them.

"Hurry!" Mr. Zanz pleaded. "This way!"

They went through a long corridor that smelled of mold and mildew. Mr. Zanz stopped at the end, handed Yosh his flashlight, and pushed aside a pile of boards that tumbled with a dreadful racket. The dust the boards raised made everyone cough. Stepping over the obstacle, they discovered a steep stairway leading underground.

"Any hiding place worthy of the name has an emergency exit," Mr. Zanz said as he replaced the boards hurriedly.

On the first step of the stairway, Linus shuddered. He thought he heard voices and a stampede in the basement, as if the police were hot on their heels. Up ahead, Mr. Zanz was rushing down the stairs.

"Go catch up with Yosh," Linus whispered to Mieg. "I'm going to help Toscane."

They let go of each other's hands. Linus turned and took Toscane by the arm. She was out of breath and unsteady on the slippery steps. She leaned on Linus to catch her balance and they went down the steps together. At the bottom of the stairs, on the right, was a drafty recess from which a heavy sugary odor escaped.

"Be ready," Mr. Zanz said. "We'll have to be quick."

"Where are we?" Toscane asked.

Mr. Zanz's flashlight was focused on his wristwatch, which he looked at intently. "In the Zip," he said. Suddenly he yelled, "Now!"

Without thinking, Linus and the others followed close on his heels. They made their way down the dark and narrow passageway, where the draft whistled and grew stronger. They heard indistinct creaking and rumbling noises. Linus put his hand over his nose. The vanilla smell! There was no mistaking the powerful, loathsome odor that was used in the trains.

At the end of the passageway, Mr. Zanz turned around.

"Trains come every two minutes!" he shouted. "Run to the left and hug the wall. There's a shelter fifty yards from here. Hurry up!"

Yosh was the first to jump down onto the tracks, followed by Mieg. Linus, sickened by the smell, couldn't breathe. When he caught up with Mr. Zanz, Linus glanced at him in panic.

"Jump, Linus!" Mr. Zanz ordered. He pushed Linus, then jumped down himself and helped Toscane.

The Zip rails glistened here and there, reflecting the small light fixtures on the walls. Linus ran, almost twisting his ankles, wide-eyed and nauseous. Finally, just as he heard the oncoming train, he felt a recess in the wall: the shelter! He flung himself into it, colliding with Yosh and Mieg, who were already huddled inside. Mr. Zanz and Toscane joined them. Two seconds later, the long, luminous Zip train whizzed by, nearly brushing against them.

"Get ready to move from here!" Mr. Zanz announced as soon as the train had passed. "To the left, on to the next shelter!"

They had to dart from recess to recess a dozen times, until they saw a brightly lit station platform behind a curve in the tunnel. Linus's lungs were on fire; he felt more dead than alive. In her growing exhaustion, Toscane perilously delayed Mr. Zanz. Just before the station platform, the tunnel widened. They barely managed to cram together on the steps of the service stairway as a train pulled out of the station. Their nerves on edge, they were completely drained.

Mr. Zanz crawled up onto the platform. "One at a time," he whispered.

Toscane climbed first, awkwardly squeezing under

the barrier, and motioned that the coast was clear. Two passengers were waiting at the other end of the platform, oblivious to the strange single file emerging from the tracks.

When they were finally all together on the platform, they were less tense, except for Linus, who was still overcome by the omnipresent vanilla odor.

"I'm sorry about all this," Mr. Zanz said. "It was dangerous, but we had no choice."

"Where are we?" Linus asked, twisting his neck to read the name of the station.

"At the end of the line."

"In the city? In the Protected Zone?"

Mr. Zanz nodded, then smiled when he noticed Linus's cheeks grow pale under the layer of black dust that covered them. "Don't worry," he said. "Protected Zone or not, you can't use your ID card anymore."

Linus repressed a wave of nausea. "No more ID card," he said in disbelief.

"If you go through the decoders, the police will locate you immediately. You're a fugitive, Linus. The zones are meaningless as far as you're concerned. The same applies to you," Mr. Zanz added, turning to Toscane. "Your father is probably on to us. He must be the one who alerted the police. If you go back to the transit home, he'll have you arrested as an accomplice."

Toscane tottered, as if she'd been punched in the stomach.

"I'll give you more details, but not here," Mr. Zanz

continued. He took Yosh and Mieg aside. "Go home immediately. You shouldn't be mixed up in any of this."

Mieg shook her head and looked at Linus with distress. "I can't!" she moaned. "I . . . We've hardly seen each other!"

"You'll see each other again very soon," Mr. Zanz assured her. "I'll keep you informed, I promise. If you want to help us, go home!"

Yosh's face was contorted by nervous tics, the prelude to another emotional crisis.

"Your whip!" Linus shouted to him as he was led away by Mr. Zanz's firm hand. "Think of your lion tamer's whip, Yosh!"

He waved to his sister, who stood transfixed on the platform with tears in her eyes. "See you soon," he mouthed.

chapter 8

Linus pinched his nose as he ran, oblivious to his sur-
roundings. The reality of the moment was eclipsed by
words lighting up in his head like garish neon signs. *Rene-*
gade. Outlaw. Fugitive. Deserter.

His legs sped on like autonomous little mechanisms,
whisking him into the unknown of the Zip's passageways,
stairs, doors, and landings. Would he have to go down
deep into the center of the earth to escape surveillance?
Entomb himself and become one of the living dead, someone with no official existence, permanently deprived of
fresh air, daylight, and spring mornings? Surprisingly,
his past vacations flashed through his mind as he ran, vacations at the beach in Florida with his grandmother. To
think that he had always been a little bored . . . If he had
only known then the true value of things, he would have
taken advantage of those happy days. When good fortune
was like a birthright, he realized, it was easy to take even
the sunshine for granted.

"Get in quick!" Mr. Zanz shouted.

Linus noticed that he was in front of a translucent elevator car. Toscane was already inside. Mr. Zanz shoved
him in.

"Where are we going?" Toscane asked, trying to catch her breath.

The elevator doors closed noiselessly. Mr. Zanz took a metal tube out of his pocket and inserted it carefully into a small hole above a digital screen. Instantly, the screen lit up. Standing on tiptoe, Mr. Zanz turned the tube slowly. A digital voice announced, "You have requested the fourth level."

Linus and Toscane stood motionless, close to each other, as the elevator rose, gathering speed. The smell of vanilla gradually faded and Linus began to breathe normally again.

"Fourth level," the voice said. "Welcome to the Eldorado Complex."

The doors opened onto a dark landing.

"Get out!" whispered Mr. Zanz. He removed the tube and jumped onto the landing after them, a split second before the elevator doors closed and it started to descend to the lower levels. He smiled. "Cheer up! We're almost there."

Linus went up to a wide glass door; on the other side, he could see a few lights. They were the shop signs, which stayed lit all night, on the energy-saving mode. "Eldorado Complex," he mumbled, trying to figure out why it sounded familiar.

"The newest suburban shopping center," Mr. Zanz said. "It sprang out of the earth, like a mushroom, eight months ago. At this hour everything is closed except the hotels."

Toscane grabbed Mr. Zanz by the sleeve. "Are you taking us to a hotel?" she asked.

"It's only a three-star Realm Two hotel," he said apologetically. "I can't offer you anything more luxurious."

"But . . . how can we . . . ?" Toscane stammered. "That's not at all . . ."

"I've been testing this hiding place for six months," Mr. Zanz said, to put her mind at rest. "It's quite safe. And very well located. You'll understand why."

He made Linus and Toscane go through a service door, which he opened with his mysterious metal tube. After they'd walked through a corridor reeking of kitchen odors, they came to another door, which Mr. Zanz knocked sharply on three times. A very tall woman with the broad shoulders of a rugby player opened the door and greeted them good-naturedly.

"My evening caller!" she said, chuckling. "I expected you later tonight!"

"We had to speed things up," Mr. Zanz explained.

"But . . . you're not alone?" the woman said, surprised.

Linus and Toscane greeted her with shy nods.

"Unforeseen circumstances, Berthalia. But I'm counting on you to . . . you know."

The woman burst into peals of laughter. "With you, never a dull moment. I'll get you what you need by tomorrow morning, I promise!" she said.

Berthalia stepped aside to let them in. Linus and Toscane discovered the scullery of a restaurant deserted by its personnel. Berthalia removed her rubber gloves and threw them into a pail filled with soapy water. "Off to paradise!" she announced as she pulled up a rolling shutter. "You'll have to squeeze in, dears!"

Linus leaned over for a closer look. He grasped Mr. Zanz's arm. "That's a dumbwaiter, isn't it?"

"Correct," Mr. Zanz replied calmly. "Unfortunately, the main entrance isn't for us. You go first. I'll help Toscane climb in."

Though astonished, Linus obeyed without a word. He climbed up onto the ledge and, crawling flat on his stomach, slid in under the shutter. He crouched at the other end while Toscane and Mr. Zanz got in. Berthalia stuck her ruddy face into the opening. "How about some delicacies as an extra? They're free!" She handed Toscane a paper bag, then winked at Linus. "Welcome to the Eldorado Complex, sweetie!"

She rolled down the shutter with a bang. The dumbwaiter creaked up in total darkness. Linus put his hands against the walls. He felt them vibrating disturbingly. When the contraption stopped, Mr. Zanz groped to release the shutter, then lifted it and got out. Linus and Toscane quickly extracted themselves from the improvised elevator too.

"Here we are!" Mr. Zanz said, delighted. "You're in my home! The best hiding place of my new organization! Paradise in the heart of hell!"

chapter 9

At that late hour, hell was asleep. In the dead of night, the countless shuttered stores, restaurants, movie theaters, game parlors, sports arenas, and auditoriums awaited daylight, when their jaws would reopen and reabsorb customers. His forehead pressed against the tinted windowpane of the hotel room, Linus gazed at the Eldorado Complex's empty pathways. He'd never been in a place that catered to the population of Realm Two. Lifting his eyes, he noticed the archways of the domed roof of the shopping center, and beyond them, almost unreal-looking, the inaccessible star-studded sky.

"Wait till tomorrow, nine o'clock, and you'll understand," Mr. Zanz said. "Thousands of people rush in there. They buy everything and anything—frenetically. After all, it's the only pleasure they still enjoy: spending their money so that they have the illusion of existing."

Linus moved away from the window.

"Want a donut?" Toscane asked, handing him the paper bag Berthalia had given them.

He declined with a weary smile and walked around the room slowly: two narrow beds, two armchairs, an adjoining bathroom. A small lamp, on the floor next to one of the beds, shed a subdued light.

"I'm sorry it doesn't have the latest modern conveniences," Mr. Zanz said. "The shower doesn't work. Neither does the automatic cleaning service. There isn't even a TV! And there's no fresh air because the windows are sealed. And the final inconvenience . . ." He went up to a door and turned the knob. ". . . is this!" he said, opening the door.

Linus was stunned. Behind the door was a wall.

"This room was boarded up by the management," Mr. Zanz explained. "It was used as a model showroom while the hotel was being built. Everything is fake! The only entrance now is through the dumbwaiter. When Berthalia told us about this room, I immediately saw how its 'inconveniences' could be turned to advantages and how perfectly they suited me." He twirled the metal tube between his fingers. "Without this master key, no one can get in or out."

Linus went up to the shower cubicle and turned the faucet. No water. He tried the various switches—hair dryer, soap dispenser. Nothing worked. Upset, he went back into the main room and sat down again. He looked at Mr. Zanz out of the corner of his eye. Mr. Zanz's hair had become whiter; he looked old and tired, but his green eyes still sparkled with intelligence.

"I'm glad to see you again," Linus said.

"Me too," Mr. Zanz said, smiling at him. "I really wish

things had worked out differently, but the main thing is you're here."

Linus nodded. "Toscane and Dr. Ambrose told me what happened on the day of the exam. Do you think the police are looking for you too?"

Mr. Zanz looked unsure. "The people who were arrested were probably questioned before being eliminated. It's very possible they named names. In any case, we have to be extremely cautious. Since that day, we've stopped using the Internet, the telephone, and messaging. Information is relayed in person. Just like in the Middle Ages! It's our revenge on progress!" His face darkened and he added, "Also, since that day I'm no longer a citizen of Realm Two—or of any realm, for that matter."

Linus felt his arms break out in goose bumps. "How is that possible?" he asked. "Everyone belongs to a realm!"

"It's possible to live differently, Linus. For a while, anyhow. But you have to be shrewd, be constantly on your guard, and hide. I've established a protocol. If it works for me, it should work for you and Toscane too. I'll explain it in detail tomorrow, once Berthalia brings us what we need."

Linus sighed, resigned. Cryptic sentences were Mr. Zanz's specialty, and after all, he had no choice but to trust him. Exhausted by the frenzied day, he stretched out on the carpet and folded his arms under his neck. He thought of the transit home. Sadko and the others were probably asleep. The next day they would be working again at their strenuous tasks on the packaging assembly line, as they would be day after day, until their release. Linus realized that he preferred the danger of his present situation to the exasperating routine of the transit home.

He extended his right leg and searched in his pocket. He took out the small vanilla tablet, sat up cross-legged, and held out his open palm in front of Mr. Zanz. Intrigued, Toscane stopped eating her donut and came closer.

"This is the tablet they asked us to take after the exam," Linus said. "Do you remember it, Toscane?"

She took the tablet between her thumb and index finger, screwed up her eyes, and shook her head. "No, I don't," she said. "I don't remember anything. When you asked us before, I tried to think back. Nothing came to mind. It's very odd: I know I took the exam, I know my score, and that's all."

Mr. Zanz knelt down near Linus and seized the pill. "What about you?" he asked. "Do you remember the exam?"

Linus nodded. "I couldn't swallow the tablet. I think that's why my memory is intact."

Mr. Zanz brought the tablet to his nose, sniffed it, then pushed his eyeglasses up to his forehead and studied it with an expert eye.

"But what reason would they have for erasing our memories?" Toscane asked, puzzled. "It's only an exam, after all. I don't feel I lived through a traumatic ordeal."

"That's just it!" Linus cried out. "You don't feel you have! That's exactly what they want!"

Mr. Zanz frowned and sat down in an armchair. He crossed his legs and looked at Linus attentively, inviting him to tell them everything. So, with relief and frustration, Linus described all that he remembered. He spoke rapidly, like a sped-up tape recording. The more images, odors, sensations, and noises he described, the paler Mr. Zanz turned.

"It was so demeaning!" Linus finally said, breathlessly. "After the exam, the examinees were all in a daze. They looked like the survivors of a natural disaster. The girl next to me had even urinated in her pants without realizing it. We were completely debilitated: human wrecks. Then the pill worked its magic. No one thought of complaining about the way they had been treated. I kept my anger bottled up inside me. I was afraid I'd seem suspicious if I talked about it." Unsteadily, Linus managed to get up and go back to the window. He pressed his forehead against the windowpane again. The contact with the cold glass had a calming effect. "Some of the images I saw on the screen were photos of me when I was little. Do you think my parents gave them the photos? Do you think they collaborated with the Great Processor?"

Formulating this horrible suspicion made him feel both relieved and guilty. How many times had he had the nightmarish vision of his parents handing the family photos to the invisible, all-powerful Great Processor?

"Are you sure it was really you in the photos?" Mr. Zanz asked after a pause.

Linus was about to reply yes when he stopped himself.

"Every child in Realm One has blown out candles on his or her birthday cake," Mr. Zanz continued. "Every child in Realm One has spent vacations by the sea. Were there any other people in the photos?"

Linus thought hard. "No. I was always alone."

"And you were under such stress. Didn't you say the images flashed by very fast? They might have shown you photos of another child—retouched, fake pictures. But they conditioned you to think you were seeing pictures of yourself. This strikes me as a much simpler explanation."

Linus was speechless. That possibility had never occurred to him. Toscane started pacing the room. "I don't understand!" she said, twisting a lock of hair. "What's the point of showing us these images and making us suffer? What are the Great Processor's computations based on?"

"Everything and nothing!" Mr. Zanz said indignantly. "So many parameters are involved that the whole thing is meaningless. From what Linus just said, I believe the exam is nothing but a form of mental torture. The sensors probably measure stress-induced chemical reactions— saliva acidity, heartbeat, nervous tension, and so on. The Great Processor probably combines this data with the student's overall grade average, taking into account his or her social background. Add to that the student's state of health, degree of resistance to pain, and—why not?— color of socks. In the end, all this results in a score."

Toscane chuckled. "You might as well be adding up carrots and turnips! What a soup!"

Linus broke into a smile. That was exactly what it was: a soup. But it was no laughing matter that everyone believed that the Great Processor's computations were fair.

"Even without your recollections, we knew this," Mr. Zanz said, more calmly. "The exam is completely arbitrary. Its sole purpose is to justify the partitioning into realms. It segregates people and makes them believe the method is scientific."

Toscane stood in the middle of the room, her hands on her hips. "But if they wipe out our memories of the exam as soon as it's over, then it's all a pointless hocus-pocus. The logic is twisted."

"Not so twisted!" Mr. Zanz whispered, looking as if his mind was racing. "If we still had memories of the exam, we would realize that we had been manipulated. Everyone would understand that the exam is worthless. There would be a revolution."

Linus moved away from the window and went up to Toscane. "I've been puzzling over this for six months," he said to her. "I'm sure you still have traces of the exam in your brain. Traces that are so deeply buried you can't access them. But the trauma must be there somewhere."

Toscane put her hands on her temples and started massaging her head vigorously, as if she had a migraine.

"I'm sure Linus is right," Mr. Zanz said. "And it's that trace that prevents most people from questioning the exam and the Great Processor. The experience they went through, all alone in the small dark cubicle, keeps their fear alive. Their minds have been stamped by a branding iron and they are prisoners of the terror engraved in their unconscious."

After a weighty silence, Mr. Zanz let out a deep sigh. "Some people must be more resistant to the exam trauma than others. Otherwise, every one of us would be subject to that fear; no one would attempt to oppose the system and my organization wouldn't exist. That's the flaw. There's always a flaw."

Half dazed, Toscane sank into the other empty armchair. Her hand trembling, she pointed to the tablet Linus had back in his hand. "And what if we found a way of preventing people from taking that thing?"

Linus shook his head and raised his arms to show his powerlessness. "It's not possible!" he moaned. "They're capable of killing people. They've arrested Dr. Ambrose and would do the same to us. Plus we're . . . we're stuck here, at the mercy of the stupid dumbwaiter. There's nothing we can do!"

He threw himself onto one of the beds and punched the mattress. "And what about Chem, all by himself in his reeducation camp? And Yosh and Mieg, and my mother, with her depression, and my father, who's ashamed of me? And you, Toscane, with your father, who sent the police after us? We can't count on anyone!"

He sprawled out on his bed and watched as Toscane went to lie down on the other. They were both completely drained.

Little by little, Linus's tired body began to relax, and

he felt terribly sleepy. Mr. Zanz came up and tucked in his blanket. Leaning over the bed, the rebel organizer said softly, "We've become citizens without ID cards, Linus. Like ghosts who no longer belong in any realm. But we have friends in each. That's our strength. With a bit of luck and a lot of persistence, one day we'll find out who's hiding behind the 'they' we've been talking about. We have to keep our hopes alive and keep fighting."

Linus and Toscane fell into a deep sleep. Mr. Zanz turned off the little lamp and settled in an armchair. To the darkness, he added, "Tomorrow I'll show you how ghosts walk through walls."

chapter 10

With a start, Linus woke to the unpleasant noise of the shutter being rolled open. He sprang up in bed, his heart pounding furiously, his mind spinning, wondering where he was. Then he saw Berthalia stooped inside the wide-open dumbwaiter, smiling at him broadly.

"How about giving me a hand?" she suggested.

Before Toscane and Mr. Zanz could get up, Linus rushed over and grabbed the woman firmly by the wrists. She managed to extract herself from the cubicle, flushed from the effort.

"Shows you how much I love you," she said, straightening herself and dusting off her overalls. She turned to take something out of the dumbwaiter. "Here! This should get you off to a good start!" She put three paper bags on one of the armchairs. Linus smelled the unpleasant odor of croissants made with margarine, but he wasn't about to be fussy that morning. For the first time in months, he was hungry. Famished, in fact.

"So? How do you like our establishment?" Berthalia inquired. "Pretty classy, isn't it?"

Toscane and Linus nodded. Their mouths were full.

Berthalia tousled their hair energetically, then went up to Mr. Zanz.

"Here, this is your breakfast!"

Mr. Zanz smiled and took the envelope she handed him. "Was it a big problem?"

"No, it was all right. But don't show up with two kids every night. My husband might eventually notice."

Mr. Zanz opened the envelope. Linus saw two little steel tubes and three plastic squares drop into his hand.

"The ID cards are no problem," Berthalia added. "They're valid for only twenty-four hours, as usual." She went to the window and yawned. "The shopping center will be opening soon. I'd better be off."

Mr. Zanz shook her hand. "Thank you so much."

"Pooh!" Berthalia chuckled. "Don't thank me. If it weren't for you, I'd be dying of boredom." Beaming, she turned to Linus and Toscane. "There's nothing worse in life than cleaning kitchens. You can't imagine how dirty they get after a day of nonstop use. But ever since I've belonged to the organization, I haven't cared. As long as I can help you, I'll clean greasy ovens every night—and even sing as I do it." She slapped her thigh, then hurried to the dumbwaiter.

"Thank you for the croissants!" Linus called out as she rolled down the shutter.

As soon as Berthalia was gone, Mr. Zanz crouched in front of them. He spread out the ID cards and steel tubes on the floor. Then he raised his eyeglasses to his receding hairline and rubbed the bridge of his nose. Once again, Linus was struck by the intelligent gleam in the man's green eyes.

"New organization, new methods," Mr. Zanz began. "We're operating within very narrow limits, but Berthalia is in a good position to help us. Her husband is a member of the Eldorado Complex security forces." He twirled one of the tubes between his fingers. "Last night Berthalia took time off from work and filched her husband's master key. She took it to a member of our network and he made these two duplicates. The tubes you see here work on all the locks within the Eldorado Complex compound: doors, elevators, and, of course, dumbwaiters." He looked meaningfully at Linus, then at Toscane.

"Understood," Linus said, reassuring Mr. Zanz. "We won't lose them."

Mr. Zanz sighed. "It would really be a nuisance. As for the ID cards . . ." He put down the tubes and tapped two of the plastic squares with his finger. "I tried to find a way of getting along without them, but couldn't."

"So we're not ghosts?" Toscane asked.

"Not really. There are too many checkpoint terminals. It's impossible to go anywhere without an ID card. But these are very special. They come directly from one of the offices of the Administration of Persons. Your friend Yosh could confirm that."

Linus almost gagged on his last piece of croissant. "You mean Yosh is providing these ID cards?"

"No, his supervisor, Mr. Kandhour."

Linus gasped. The old organization had had many members, mostly agitators who had organized strikes in the Subterranean Industrial Zone; the new organization seemed even more extensive and powerful, in spite of the heavy police surveillance.

"Whenever someone dies," Mr. Zanz continued, "their ID card is sent to the Administration of Persons. Before the card is destroyed, all the facts about the dead person's past have to be checked, classified, and categorized. This work is done very quickly because everything is digitized. That's why the cards are valid for only one day. It's another one of those tiny flaws in their perfect system. We might as well take advantage of it."

Linus stared at the plastic squares. "We're using dead people's ID cards?"

"That's right. They're blank but they work. The beauty of it is they don't transmit identification data: no photo, no date, no genetic imprint."

"So in fact we are like ghosts," Toscane concluded in a subdued voice.

She looked at Linus. He smiled. Suddenly he felt intoxicated by the thought of being an outlaw, a deserter, a ghost. Of being able to see the world not as neat separate compartments, but as a single entity, an expanse of complete freedom.

"This isn't so bad," he said, getting up and going to the window. Through the soundproof glass, he saw that the Eldorado Complex had come to life. Hundreds of people were moving about the shopping center, drawn by the neon signs announcing special offers. The fountains were turned on too. So were the automatic cleaning machines; they glided along the pathways in a strange, silent ballet. Way up near the ceiling, a giant plasma screen attached to the dome by transparent ropes broadcast commercials. Between the commercials, the face of a smiling, welcoming man appeared on the screen, along with a flashing message: *Olf Bradman, founder of the shopping center, wishes you a bargain-filled day!* Linus let himself be hypnotized momentarily by this paternal face. "Can we really go anywhere?" he asked, finally snapping out of his reverie.

"Anywhere," Mr. Zanz confirmed. "I told you: the zones are meaningless for us now. Though today there's a problem." Mr. Zanz turned to Toscane. "I'm afraid your father might already have e-mailed your photos to the police squads."

Toscane scowled and shook her head, visibly upset. "My father never wastes any time reporting the tiniest incident. So . . ."

Linus stiffened. He had an ID card, a master key, freedom . . . and he was going to be told not to go out?

"If you leave the shopping center area, your identities might be checked," Mr. Zanz continued. "The police units are bound to be mobilized for two escapees like you, particularly in the Zip. You should definitely not go out for the time being. I'm sorry."

Toscane nodded, but Linus stamped his feet in anger.

"If you're cautious, you can walk around the Eldorado Complex," Mr. Zanz said, to console him. "It's better than nothing." He put his hand on Linus's shoulder. "I can move around freely. I have to get in contact with certain members of the organization again. They'll fill me in on the measures taken by the police. By tonight we'll know what's what and we'll consider courses of action, I promise. In the meantime . . . please don't do anything foolish, okay?"

Instead of promising anything, Linus groaned sulkily and dug into a bag for another croissant. Now Toscane went to the window.

"We won't have trouble finding things to keep us busy here," she said with enthusiasm. "I haven't been to the movies in months."

Reassured, Mr. Zanz walked to the dumbwaiter and ducked under the shutter. "I'm counting on you. Please be prudent. See you tonight!"

Linus finished eating in silence while Toscane slipped into the bathroom. Alone in the silent room, Linus brooded, feeling deeply frustrated. When Toscane returned, her hair vaguely redone, she dashed to the window and asked, almost joyfully, "So, what movie do you want to see?"

"None," Linus replied.

"Would you rather go to GameSpace?"

"No."

"To the sports club?"

"Pfff!"

"You're no fun," Toscane complained. "You don't feel like doing anything."

"Yes, there is one thing I feel like doing," Linus retorted. "In fact, I've been dreaming of it for six months."

"What's that?" Toscane asked suspiciously.

"Going home."

She laughed to cover up her anxiety. "Linus . . . we promised Mr. Zanz we wouldn't leave the Eldorado Complex."

"Do what you want," he said, getting up and walking to the dumbwaiter. "I know how I'm going to spend my day."

chapter 11

"Don't look at me that way," Linus whispered, nudging Toscane with his elbow. "We're ghosts, remember? And I didn't force you to come with me."

"If our identities are checked, your day of freedom will turn ugly," Toscane shot back angrily.

The train stopped and Linus leaned to see the platform. "Look," he said. "There isn't a cop in sight."

Linus knew the place by heart. He could have found his way in his sleep: step out of the train, walk to the end of the platform, and when you reach the billboard, swipe your ID card at the gate.

But that day, when he reached the end of the platform, he felt apprehensive. His mouth was dry as he slipped his ID card into the slot and waited.

"Authorized access," the synthetic voice said soberly.

Linus hurried through. Toscane went through as well and joined him, her hands trembling. The ID cards were working; that was the main thing.

There were very few people in the station concourse, and Toscane and Linus were alone in the elevator. Once outside, in the open air, they looked at each other, half dazed.

"You see? Everything's going smoothly," Linus remarked. "Mr. Zanz gets too uptight sometimes."

In the Protected Zone's cocoonlike stillness, even their footfalls on the sidewalk seemed muffled. Linus felt as if he were floating. The tall, bare trees, tastefully decked with strings of Christmas lights, lined the spotless broad walkways. Nothing had changed. The houses were still surrounded by their large gardens, benefiting from the same air quality, quiet, and safety as before. In the cold, dry December weather, nothing moved. Linus was thoroughly familiar with the habits of the residents. At that hour of the day, they were snugly inside their houses, sitting around roasts cooked with butter and discussing their Christmas preparations.

"There's no better place on earth, is there?" he said, half nostalgic, half cynical.

Toscane walked by his side, looking queasy. Gradually, as they moved through the quiet streets, she became more relaxed. "My father never wanted to live in the Protected Zone," she said. "He prefers the apartment given to him at the transit home. He's so obsessed with his work that he can't tear himself away. He has to watch over everything constantly. This was a bone of contention between him and my mother when she was alive."

Linus balanced himself as he walked along the curb. Sensing her sadness, he waited for her to continue talking.

"I've always been convinced that my mother died of grief." Toscane sighed. "As Realm One citizens, we were entitled to every privilege, but my father never wanted anything. No vacations, no leisure activities, nothing. He's always lived solely for the transit home, ferreting out people's mistakes, supervising and guaranteeing the home's sacrosanct security. I'm sure he detected a problem as soon as Dr. Ambrose removed your bracelet. He sees everything. He's a deranged person. You can understand why I never considered following in his footsteps."

"You deserve a lot better."

"Better, I don't know. Something different, anyhow. That's why I started working for Mr. Zanz and joined his organization."

Linus held out his hand. "Come, I'll show you my house." Feeling elated, he started to run, leading Toscane down the small private streets and through covered alleyways, safe from unwelcome eyes.

He slowed down and came to a halt in front of a privet hedge. Standing on tiptoe, he saw the roof of his house. From that spot, none of the neighbors could see them. Linus parted the branches and looked at the garden. The morning frost had melted. Droplets glistened on the blades of grass. Linus stifled a cry. On the terrace, looking out at the trees and the pale sky, his mother was taking a breath of air. She was muffled up in her coat, motionless, and alone.

Toscane pulled him back. "What's wrong?" she whispered.

Linus was speechless. There was his mother, fifteen yards away from him. Then the terrace door opened and Mieg appeared. She went up to their mother quietly. From that distance, it seemed to Linus that they were both the same height. Mieg might even be a bit taller than Mrs. Hoppe.

With a lump in his throat, Linus saw Mieg kiss their mother's cheek, snapping her from a deep reverie. Then Mrs. Hoppe let her daughter lead her back into the house. The terrace door closed behind them. Linus didn't dare move. This painful and marvelous apparition left him paralyzed.

"What are we doing now?" Toscane asked impatiently, standing behind him.

Linus stepped back from the hedge, his eyes clouded with tears.

"You shouldn't have come," Toscane whispered. "It's too hard on you."

Linus caught his breath and gulped repeatedly. His head was throbbing like a pump. Being there, so close to happiness, had jolted him, and he was now acutely aware of the absurdity of the situation.

"I have to see my mother," he said. "I have to tell her that I'm alive, that I'm free, that I love her."

Toscane grabbed his shoulders and shook him. "You can't do that! It's too risky! What if your mother informs against us? Think about the consequences."

Linus clenched his teeth and gave Toscane a withering look. "My mother wouldn't inform against us! She needs to see me. Just as I need to see her."

"What makes you so sure?" Toscane said angrily.

"My mother isn't like your father!"

He pushed her away harshly, turned, and plunged into the privet hedge. He extricated himself from the branches and ran noiselessly up to the house, where he leaned on the wall and closed his eyes momentarily to calm his throbbing heart.

Then he walked stealthily along the wall until he reached the terrace at the back of the house. Everything was quiet in the surrounding area. Several crows cawed in the trees and flew above the shack where his father stored logs every autumn. He stepped onto the terrace and walked up close to the French windows. There he leaned forward boldly and peered inside.

The entire Hoppe family was gathered in the living room. His mother was sitting on the couch with her back to him. Linus could make out Mieg's dark hair next to her. Mr. Hoppe was standing and passing drinks around. He handed someone a glass, and Linus had to lean forward slightly to see who it was: a slender, silver-haired woman. "Grandma?" he whispered. It was her! His grandmother had come for the holidays. Overcome with emotion, Linus felt his knees weaken. He looked away and leaned back against the wall. They were all there, so close to him. He could easily be with them, where he belonged. All he had to do was walk into the living room and sit down, and the family circle would be complete. Why not? Why wasn't he allowed to do so? Why should an exam grade have the power to deprive him of his family's affection? Linus slumped down to the ground, his back against the wall. Tears welled up in his eyes.

At that moment, a noise startled him. Someone had opened the French windows. He threw himself flat on the ground and quickly began to crawl out of sight. Just as he was nearly invisible, hidden behind a corner of the wall, he heard a voice ask, "How many should I get, Mr. Hoppe?"

"Three or four," Linus's father replied from the living room. Then he added, "Please, Yosh, I told you: call me Tobias."

"I'll try, Mr. . . . I mean, Tobias."

Curled up on the cold ground, Linus felt as if an arrow had just pierced his heart. He bit his lips so that he wouldn't scream. Yosh! Yosh was there too! It was Saturday and he was about to eat lunch with the Hoppe family. Linus's family. Did that mean that Yosh was living there, in Linus's house?

Linus waited for a minute, then crawled back to the corner to look. He saw Yosh crossing the garden and opening the shack. Linus smoothed his hand over his forehead. His face was burning. Just as Yosh turned, Linus stood up and made his presence known. Yosh uttered a cry and dropped the logs he was carrying. They fell with a crash and rolled onto the terrace.

"Yosh!" Mr. Hoppe called through the half-open door.
"Is everything all right?"

Without taking his eyes off Linus, Yosh answered in a surprised, choked voice, "Yes, yes. . . . I stumbled. It's nothing!" Then he whispered, "You're crazy to come here!"

Linus looked him up and down with resentment. Yosh crouched down slowly to pick up the logs.

"This is my house," Linus muttered, his fists clenched. "I can come whenever I want!"

From the living room, Mr. Hoppe asked, "Do you need help?"

"No, no!" Yosh shouted back. "I can manage!"

His mouth twisted with anger and jealousy, Linus exclaimed, " 'Manage' is an understatement! You're quite an operator! We talked about swapping exam scores . . . not families! I hope you find my bed comfortable!"

Yosh lowered his eyes and started picking up the scattered logs. He fumbled and the wood slipped out of his trembling hands. "I wanted to tell you the other night," he groaned, "but we didn't have time. Mieg persuaded your parents to take me in. Please don't be mad at me. I . . . I'm not trying to take your place."

"You're not trying, but you have."

Yosh shook his head. "No, Linus, no. Your family isn't mine. You can't say—"

Linus, seething with rage, went through a list. "My bed, my house, my family, an internship at the Administration of Persons. You lost no time in slipping into the mold!"

Yosh fell to his knees, deeply hurt. "Don't criticize me for that," he pleaded. "I only joined the Administration of Persons to find my brother. And Chem. I promise. I'm not doing this to go against you."

"What's going on, Yosh?" a voice asked.

Unexpectedly, Grandma appeared on the terrace.

She paused uncertainly. It was a peculiar moment—a moment when everything seemed to switch into slow motion. Grandma's gaze went from Yosh to the scattered logs. Then she turned to Linus, who didn't have time to hide. Grandma's blue eyes, wide with surprise, were riveted on him. He felt as if something was exploding inside him: his heart bursting in his chest.

A second later, his grandmother's hands were gently but firmly pushing him back behind the corner of the house. Then she wrapped her arms around him. "Thank God, Linus!" she said, with a sob in her voice. She fondled his face. "Your parents must not see you right away. It would be too big of a shock."

She turned to Yosh and motioned for him to go back inside. "Wait one second," she said to Linus. She left him and disappeared into the house. Dazed, Linus covered his eyes with his hands. Grandma returned a minute later, her coat thrown over her shoulders.

"I told them I was going to get a breath of air," she mumbled. "Come."

She guided him to the other side of the house, to the steps leading down to the basement. As he went inside, Linus touched the walls to make sure it wasn't a dream. His house! He was home!

"You can't imagine how happy I am to see you," Grandma whispered. "No one had any idea where you were. Since I've been back, I've been moving heaven and earth to try to find you."

"Did you leave Florida?"

"Of course! I felt so useless over there."

Linus bit his lips so as not to cry. His leaving had caused so many upheavals. Grandma hugged him again.

"I came over here without really thinking," Linus explained. "I badly needed to see you all."

Grandma stepped away and looked at him sadly. "You can't just turn up like this without warning," she said. "Your mother is in a very fragile state. Give me time to lay the groundwork." Suddenly she put her finger against her lips and craned her neck to listen to the noises coming from the living room. In a low voice, she asked Linus how he had managed to enter the Protected Zone.

"It's complicated. I ran away from the home where I was locked up. I can't tell you the details."

"Then don't tell me anything."

Linus went down a few steps into the basement. He saw

equipment he had never seen there before lying on a square of carpeting—a rowing apparatus, a bodybuilding machine, a downhill-skiing simulator, and dumbbells.

Grandma sighed. "It's your father. He's developed a passion for sports. Ever since you left, he's had to let off steam." She kicked a stack of dumbbells. "He tries to numb his sorrow by working up a sweat. Silly, isn't it?"

Linus let out a small laugh. Grandma sat down on the bodybuilding machine and smiled. "Do you remember when we last spoke? Even at a distance of four thousand miles, I could tell the exam was not going to go as expected. But you seemed determined and sure of which path to take."

Linus nodded. Grandma had always been perceptive; she had always been able to read his mind.

"I suppose Mieg knew about your decision. And Yosh? This boy isn't here by chance either, is he?"

Linus held back tears and admitted mournfully, "I didn't expect Yosh to come and live here. When I saw him on the terrace, I felt like he . . . he had stolen my life."

Grandma's eyes misted over. "Don't you dare have such thoughts, do you hear? No one can ever replace you, Linus. No matter what you did, no matter what you do, we love you."

Linus hoisted himself onto the bodybuilding machine. It was strange being there with his grandmother.

"You've always been opposed to the exam, haven't you?" he asked her.

"You noticed?" Grandma chuckled. "I had endless arguments with your father about it. Now that you've been assigned to Realm Two, I'm sure he's changed his mind. He can't possibly believe in the legitimacy of this absurd system anymore."

Linus heaved a deep sigh. "I was selfish. I never thought about how this would affect all of you." He rested his head on Grandma's shoulder and she caressed his hair gently.

"Don't have any regrets. You followed your conscience, right? How can we help you? What are your plans?"

Linus looked at his grandmother; he felt relieved at her words. Questions were spinning in his head, like moths around a circle of light. "I don't know yet what I'll do," he said. "But I'm not alone, in any case."

He thought of Toscane, who was waiting for him on the other side of the hedge; she was probably frozen to the bone. It was true he wasn't alone: there were Mr. Zanz, Berthalia, and the whole network of people working for the cause, not to mention Chem and Sadko. Those people were his plans! And possibly all the other people—the ones who would be taking the exam in the next few months and were unaware of the violent treatment awaiting them. His chest bursting, Linus clasped Grandma tightly in his arms.

"Tell Yosh I'm not mad at him," he mumbled. "I was taken by surprise. Actually, it's good that he's here with Mieg."

"I'll tell him."

"And Mom . . ."

"I'll handle it. As soon as I feel she's ready, I'll tell her I saw you. I promise."

Linus jumped down from the machine, kissed his grandmother on the cheek, and headed toward the stairs. A milky segment of sky floated above the garden. Nostalgically, he watched the clouds go by. Before the exam, he had felt at home there; whereas that day he was like those clouds—just passing through.

He hoped to come back one day to see his parents, freely and openly, with Chem. In a different world, that would surely be possible. Now that he thought about it, that was his plan: to live in a different world. He turned to Grandma one last time. He felt as if she had breathed strength into him. "I'll be back soon," he said, and ran outside with a lighter heart.

chapter 13

Toscane, hidden behind the hedge, was stamping her feet. Her cheeks and nose were red.

"I almost left!" she thundered. "What were you up to? Mr. Zanz will be furious when he finds out how many risks you took."

"How will he find out?" Linus asked, removing a twig that had stuck to her sleeve.

Toscane shrugged. Her eyes shone like two pieces of incandescent coal, and anger gave her face a special glow. Linus found her almost pretty.

"I wonder what you looked like when you were thinner," he said.

Disconcerted, Toscane looked away and frowned. "Let's not hang around here. Let's go back to the station right away."

Linus took a last look at his house before starting to retrace his steps. True, it had been risky to go there. But talking to Grandma had done him a lot of good. In fact, things were not as complicated as Mr. Zanz claimed. As he walked across the lawn, he was suddenly in an excellent mood.

By the time they reached the station area, Toscane had

recovered her sense of humor. She made funny faces, trying to show him what she had looked like when she had been forty pounds lighter. She sucked in her cheeks, pulled the skin under her eyes, held her stomach in, and groaned grotesquely.

"Frankly, I like you better now," Linus said between peals of laughter.

Toscane stiffened. Still giggling, Linus nudged her. "I said I like . . ."

Seeing her go pale, he fell silent and turned toward the station. There, at the entrance to the elevators, two men with police badges on their chests were checking the identities of the passengers. They were busy with a group of young people and hadn't yet noticed Toscane and Linus.

"Turn back," Toscane whispered. "Not too fast. It has to look natural."

Breathless from the unexpected jolt, they swiveled around and began walking in the opposite direction. It was important to remain calm and not run or make noise. Linus's mind raced: how could they escape? He saw only one course of action: going back to Grandma. He whispered, "Follow me."

Toscane walked by his side, her neck stiff from fear. They turned right and ran across the lawn path again. Just as they were approaching the Hoppe residence, they saw an ecopropulsion vehicle pulling up in front of the house. Linus drew Toscane behind a thicket, where they hid, terrified. No one but the police, on orders from headquarters, had the right to drive into the residential areas of the Protected Zone. Indeed, when the vehicle had come to a stop, they saw two policemen climb out.

"They're going to my house!" Linus whispered, looking through the branches. "They're going up to the gate."

"Well then, we're done for," Toscane groaned. "They've got us cornered."

Linus grasped her hand and squeezed it hard. An idea had just occurred to him.

"No," he said. "There's still a way out."

He led Toscane back across the lawn, to a deserted lane. As they hugged the wall of a large property with discreetly lit windows, Linus had the fleeting sensation that someone was watching them from behind a curtain.

"Should we run?" Toscane asked.

"Now, yes!"

They dashed straight ahead hand in hand. Spurred by fear, they ran as fast as they could. Toscane stumbled. At the end of the street, they tore down some stairs, cut through a stretch of waterlogged grass, and reached the bottom of a hill, their shoes heavy with mud. Toscane stopped, bent in two, her hands on her thighs. She had lost her breath.

"Do you really know where to go?" she asked worriedly.

"I can't guarantee anything, but . . . over there, on the other side of the hill."

They climbed up together, skidding with every step. At the top of the hill was a long, seemingly impassable barrier made of wood panels.

"Mieg and I used to come here a lot," Linus explained. "It's a soundproofing wall dating from the days of gasoline cars. Come and see."

Farther down, behind a grove of hazel trees, they discovered a breach between two broken panels. Since cars were silent now, it had been deemed unnecessary to repair the panels. On the other side of the wall was the open-air segment of a boulevard just before it disappeared underground. Linus squeezed through the narrow breach and pulled Toscane through. She grazed her forehead and almost tore her coat on the splinters of the fence. At that moment, a car emerged from the nearby parking lot where the citizens of the Protected Zone kept their vehicles. According to the ecoplan regulations, they were allowed to use their cars only on exceptional occasions. The car drove off.

"This boulevard is a way out of the Protected Zone," Linus explained. "We stand a chance."

"Are you saying we should hitchhike?"

"Do you have any other suggestions?"

"What if we end up with someone who knows you?"

"We'll see. We'll play it by ear!"

"What if no one stops for us?"

Linus started walking down to the boulevard. "We have no choice!" he called out.

Toscane followed him without conviction.

The boulevard was deserted. On one side were the gates to the parking lot entrance; on the other was the gaping tunnel entrance. They stood at the periphery of the road, waiting for the next car. An icy wind was blowing and the last dead leaves swirled on the asphalt. Everything was silent. The parking lot gates remained shut. *If only I'd been told that one day I'd be a prisoner in the Protected Zone!* thought Linus, half amused, half bitter.

Demoralized, Toscane shook her head. "I should have stopped you from leaving the hotel room this morning. I should have knocked you unconscious. If we get arrested, it'll be my fault."

"We're not going to get arrested. We're going to get out of here. We just have to wait for the next car."

Toscane fell into a stubborn silence.

"I don't regret having come here," Linus went on. "I needed to. Look at my neck! The swelling is nearly gone. Dr. Ambrose was right: freedom was the cure."

He walked a few steps down the road. Then, returning to Toscane's side, he asked her, "Tell me, what was it like in the reeducation camp? Every time I ask, you avoid answering."

Toscane shrank back in an odd way, then crossed her arms and said, "This is hardly the time to talk about that."

"I think it is! Tonight I'm going to ask Mr. Zanz to find a way for me to join Chem. The organization needs him as much as it needs me."

The wind had picked up and Toscane's teeth started chattering. She walked in circles and stomped her feet a few times to warm up. Finally she stood in front of Linus and took a deep breath. "It's impossible to get your friend Chem out of Realm Three," she said.

Linus was skipping along the edge of the boulevard. "Why? The organization seems to me even more powerful than it was."

"Mr. Zanz will say the same thing," Toscane continued. "It's impossible! Completely impossible!"

Linus stood still. "It's not impossible!" he shouted. "I'll get him out of that penal colony no matter what it takes."

Toscane was about to shout back when they were startled by a noise coming from the other side of the wall. They raised their heads. All of a sudden, Linus saw the red hat with the insignia of the Higher Institute of Architecture emerging from between the two broken boards, and, under the hat, Mieg's worried face.

"Thank heavens you're here!" she exclaimed.

They watched, astounded, as she tumbled down toward them.

"The police are looking for you everywhere," Mieg said. "They turned up at home, and they're questioning Dad. You're crazy to have come!" She looked at Linus and winked. "It's a good thing I know my kid brother. I immediately thought of our secret passageway."

She turned toward the parking lot. Linus and Toscane swiveled around. The gates opened and a car appeared. Mieg jumped into the middle of the roadway and began to make frantic signals.

The car halted in front of them. Linus couldn't distinguish the traits of the driver behind the tinted windshield. The rear door opened with a clicking sound.

"Get in quickly," Mieg urged them. "The police will probably seal off the entire zone."

Stunned, Linus and Toscane climbed into the car. Mieg slammed the door and remained alone on the road. Linus felt arms around him, clasping him so tightly he almost choked. A perfume he had known all his life entered his nostrils.

"Mom?" he mumbled.

"Linus," Mrs. Hoppe said, sighing as the car pulled away.

From the driver's seat, Grandma said, "See? I kept my promise, Linus. But I had to do it a bit sooner than expected: when I saw the police at our doorstep, I had no choice but to explain to your mother why I needed her car so urgently."

chapter 14

For a while, Linus felt as if he were floating in another world, outside space and time. He was just a child snuggled in his mother's arms, surrounded by her warmth, protected from any outside aggression. All he could hear was her heart beating against his ear. Nothing else existed—not Grandma, Toscane, the car, the tunnel, the police. A marvelous feeling of happiness spread inside him.

Mrs. Hoppe broke the silence. "Forgive me," she whispered. "I had no idea. I didn't understand."

Linus pulled out of her embrace and looked at her with tears in his eyes, unable to say a word. Mrs. Hoppe scrutinized her son's distressed face.

"I found an album in Mieg's closet," she said.

Linus bit his tongue. The album contained his correspondence with Yosh before the exam.

"I know I shouldn't have pried," Mrs. Hoppe said apologetically, "but I couldn't help it. Your absence made me suffer so much. I couldn't stand not having an explanation. I'd already searched your room, but it was only this morning that I came across the album." She opened her lined jumpsuit and extracted a big envelope. She smiled. "It's a good thing I kept it on me. If the police had come across it . . ."

Linus seized the envelope. The album was in there, dog-eared from having been leafed through so often. And inside were the photos, the printed messages, all the evidence of his swap plan with Yosh.

"I had a shock discovering the plan you and Yosh had concocted," Mrs. Hoppe went on. "I went out on the terrace afterward and stared into space for a long time." She squeezed Linus's arm. "In the end, I felt proud."

"Proud?" Linus said, astonished, his voice hoarse with emotion.

Mrs. Hoppe nodded. Her face, lit by the neon lights in the tunnel, flickered like an image in an old movie. "Six or seven months ago, I wouldn't have understood why you wanted to change realms. I had never questioned the fairness of our system. I just took advantage of it. Since I was on the right side, I thought that I deserved the position I had, and that the others, the people in Realm Two, had no right to complain of their fates. Everything was as it should be: the powerful on one side, the weak on the other, the two well segregated from each other. And then you vanished and I thought I'd die of despair. Our neighbors, our friends, everyone began to regard us with a kind of pity . . . or disgust. A son in Realm Two! What a disgrace! But I still loved and admired you. So I realized we lived in a less-than-perfect world. And that's when Yosh moved in with us. At first I couldn't get used to his presence. I found him odd. With time, I got to know him better, and he told me about his life in Realm Two with his parents. This gave me more doubts. No one deserves to live like that!" She caught her breath and continued. "When I read the messages pasted in the album, I understood that you felt you were suffocating in Realm One and didn't feel free to do as you pleased. And I realized we never discussed your wishes or desires. Your father and I were so sure we were offering you the best, we forgot to listen to you." She put her trembling hand over her mouth. "We certainly learned the hard way, you know."

Linus held out his arms to his mother to console her. But he met Toscane's somber gaze and checked his gesture out of consideration to her. "I missed you," he said simply, taking his mother's hand.

"We'll soon be exiting the tunnel," Grandma announced. "We'd better know where we're going." She stared at Linus from the rearview mirror.

He smiled at her. "Thank heavens you were quick," he said with a sigh of relief.

"You should thank Yosh and Mieg. As soon as they saw the police in front of the house, they made me escape from the far end of the garden. And your mother followed me. Your father must have been flabbergasted! A search, can you imagine? At the home of an executive of the Economic Observatory. It's completely unheard of."

Toscane was beginning to get impatient. She shifted in her seat, twisting a lock of hair. "Drive us to the Eldorado Complex," she said to Grandma. "It's in the Open Zone; our identities won't be checked."

Mrs. Hoppe leaned toward Toscane, surprised. "The Eldorado Complex? Why? What for?"

Toscane hesitated, not knowing whether to answer, and exchanged glances with Linus.

"Don't go there," Mrs. Hoppe said. "It's the worst possible place. They're looking for you. You won't get by the cameras."

"You know this shopping center?" Linus said, puzzled. "It's for Realm Two people."

Mrs. Hoppe wrung her hands. "I designed the video surveillance system. Remember? I was working on this building site last spring. The complex opened just before the exam."

Linus knocked his fist against his forehead. That was why the name had seemed familiar to him. He had heard it mentioned at home, during dinner conversations. It was obvious! But at the time, he had been so obsessed with his own problems that the name hadn't sunk in.

"So?" Grandma asked impatiently. "Where to?"

The car emerged on a streamlined suspension bridge spanning the Seine River. At the end of the bridge was the junction of several roads.

"To the Eldorado Complex!" Linus said decisively. He turned to his mother. "That's where we have to go. Someone is waiting for us and we have passkeys."

Mrs. Hoppe nodded and turned toward the window. They drove through a kind of Plexiglas tube, beyond which were the blurred contours of trees and buildings and, below, the banks of the river. Though it was nightfall, and the winter light made the landscape a bit melancholy, it still would have been a tempting spot to take a quiet stroll and relax.

"You can't turn back the clock," Mrs. Hoppe said in a barely audible voice. A tear rolled down her cheek. "You'll never be able to come home and live with us again. What's going to become of you, Linus?"

He put his hand on her cheek and let the tear move onto his finger, as he used to do with ladybugs when he was little. "I have no idea what will become of me. That's true. But I have friends who are counting on me. I've got to do everything I can to help them."

"Chem?" Mrs. Hoppe asked in a broken voice.

"Yes. And Sadko Flavitch, who's stuck in the transit home where I've lived and worked for the past six months." The tear glistened on Linus's fingertip. He looked at the quivering drop of salt water and wondered foolishly if it would fly away. "For six months," he went on, "I loaded and unloaded cartons on a packaging assembly line. I thought I'd go crazy. If Toscane hadn't been there . . ." The tear rolled down his finger and vanished in the lines of his palm. "Don't worry," he said. "One day I'll come back home."

They had just driven into the covered parking lot of the shopping center. Grandma programmed the automatic steering wheel to find a parking space. It was the end of the afternoon and customers were leaving the Eldorado Complex in droves, their car trunks filled with objects both indispensable and superfluous. Mrs. Hoppe lifted her eyes and looked through the slits of the vaulted parking lot ceiling at the skyscraper dominating the complex.

"I worked here for several months," she said pensively, "at a time when everything was going well. I was proud of having designed the surveillance system for such a huge, busy place. When my work assignment came to an end, the boss, Olf Bradman, was so pleased, he invited me to his home for dinner with his wife and son. What an honor!" She burst out laughing, her hand over her mouth. "You should have seen it, Linus. That man lives in a palace. And his thirteen-year-old son already sees himself as a big boss. He told me all about a project he was implementing to handle certain types of delinquents. He spoke like the head of a company, with self-confidence and contempt. His father was so proud of him. I'd like to see Bradman's face if his kid gets flunked and assigned to Realm Two!" She stopped laughing. There was an embarrassed silence inside the car.

"You understand, Linus," Mrs. Hoppe went on, "I believed it all. I thought I was making a contribution to the perfect structure of our society. Why do we spy on people? To enforce security! For everyone's good—and the misfortune of outlaws, thieves, rioters, drug and arms traffickers . . . And now my cameras are going to spy on you. They are going to stalk you and unmask you. And if everything works as I planned, you'll be caught and arrested by the police." She stopped. An idea seemed to have occurred to her. She leaned toward Grandma.

"Go park over there," she said. "Near the gray door. Do you see it?"

Grandma switched the car back into manual control. "Here?" she asked.

Mrs. Hoppe nodded. "Yes, that's good. If I remember accurately, this door gives access to passageways for the firemen. We didn't put cameras inside them." She turned to Linus, her eyes filled with hope. "You should be able to open the door with your passkey. Trust me; go this way!"

The car unlocked automatically and the doors opened.

"I'll contact Yosh and Mieg as soon as I can," Linus promised. "You'll hear from me."

Toscane pulled him by the sleeve. He stepped out of the car, feeling deeply torn. He sent his mother and grandmother kisses from the other side of the window, then joined Toscane, who was already turning the metallic tube in the lock of the gray door.

chapter 15

"My little darlings!" Berthalia greeted them. She took off her rubber gloves and dashed to the rolling shutter. "Get in fast! Mr. Zanz is waiting for you. But first give me your ID cards. I'll get you two new ones tomorrow morning."

Linus and Toscane complied, and Berthalia helped them climb into the dumbwaiter. Just as she was about to roll down the shutter, her face lit up with a warm smile. "Feeling a little hungry after your day of freedom?"

Toscane grimaced. "Not tonight, thank you."

"Then up you go to paradise!"

● ● ●

In the room, Mr. Zanz welcomed them, looking relieved. "Where were you?" he asked curtly.

"At the movies," Toscane replied.

Mr. Zanz frowned, looked hard at them, and breathed a resigned sigh. Then he started pacing around the room, his hands in his pockets. Linus lay down on his bed. He felt almost as tired as after a day of work in the STZ, with one difference: this evening, the aching muscle was his heart. The anxious faces of his mother, his grandmother, and Mieg haunted him and he couldn't shake off a deep feeling of gloom.

"I dropped in on one of the members of the organization," Mr. Zanz began. "According to his sources, Toscane's father has given out descriptions of both of you, and your photos have been broadcast throughout the security system."

Toscane laughed nervously. "Thanks a lot, Dad!"

Mr. Zanz dug into a bag and took out a bottle of water. He offered it to Linus and Toscane, then drank greedily, straight from the bottle, like someone who hadn't had any liquid intake for days.

"Dr. Ambrose was cross-examined by the police all night," he continued, wiping his mouth. "We tried to find out where she was, but . . ." He fell silent. His hands were trembling. Finally he added, "In the late afternoon we heard that her ID card had been sent to the Administration of Persons."

Linus struggled to sit up on his bed. Had he understood correctly the meaning of what had been said? He glanced at Toscane despairingly. "Does this mean Dr. Ambrose is dead?" he asked in a choked voice.

Mr. Zanz raised his arms and lowered them helplessly. All his anger, impotence, and anguish could be read in that simple gesture.

"Children, we've entered a particularly difficult phase," he said. "Dr. Ambrose's death confirms our worst fears. The police forces have become uncompromising. Their goal is clear: they're out to destroy every form of dissent. As soon as they suspect someone of acting against the system, they kill them."

These last words cracked in Linus's ears like the lash of a whip.

"The whole organization is in danger," Mr. Zanz went on, "whatever the level of responsibility of its members. For once there's no discrimination: citizens of Realm One and citizens of Realm Two are equal and the punishment is the same for all. Death."

Stunned, Linus curled up on the bed. His mind was spinning. *How far am I willing to go?* he asked himself. *Am I prepared to die for the organization?* He seemed to be living in an upside-down world. A powerful, extensive, faceless force was at work, crushing those who opposed it. He sat up abruptly, a lump in his throat, his eyes flashing with anger. "I thought your operation was working smoothly," he said. "I thought that we were safe and that we could move around freely and take action. And now you're telling me the exact opposite. The new organization isn't as powerful as you implied."

He jumped up from the bed and went to the armchair where Mr. Zanz was sitting. "You made me escape from the home, yet you knew I'd be in greater danger outside." Then, seething with rage, he turned to Toscane. "What did you expect from me? I told you everything I know about the exam. I showed you the tablet that erases memories. What more can I do?"

Toscane, tears welling up in her eyes, shook her head without saying a word.

"Our sole intention was to protect you," Mr. Zanz replied. "If you'd stayed at the home, you'd have been at the mercy of the police."

"Here or there, what's the difference?" Linus cried out with bitterness. "Anyhow, you can't protect me anymore."

Mr. Zanz got up, walked to the wall, and leaned his forehead against it. "Obviously we have no choice," he said calmly. "The only thing we can still do is sabotage the next exam. That will weaken the system, perhaps even shatter it. It's our only chance." He turned and looked at Linus. "We must find out who's hiding behind the Great Processor. It's not just a machine! Clearly it was conceived and programmed by human beings. We have to expose them, for they're the ones who give out the orders and impose a reign of terror."

"Even if it means being arrested and meeting the same fate as Dr. Ambrose?" Linus asked, his teeth clenched.

"Yes."

Linus shook his head. "You can't force me to put my life on the line. It's easier for you. You're an adult; you don't have a family. . . ."

Mr. Zanz winced and stepped back as if he'd been socked in the stomach. His features expressed deep distress. "I didn't have that piece of luck," he said. "I invented a family for myself, built it from scratch. It consists of my friends, the members of my organization. And you're among them, Linus." He paused. "I'm not gambling with your life," he added, trembling with emotion. "If you have to vent your anger on someone, vent it on the people who built this unjust world we're fighting against. Not on me."

Contrite, Linus retreated to the window. A heavy silence fell over the small room.

Behind the tinted windowpane, the Eldorado Complex's Christmas garlands, neon signs, overstocked shops, and giant plasma screen with Olf Bradman's smiling face overlooking it all seemed like a provocation. Linus clenched his fists. How much simpler and easier it would have been to be an obedient Realm Two citizen. For a few seconds, he imagined himself going down the aisles, from store to store, happy that he could buy himself trinkets with his savings. If only that were sufficient in life. But no, it was an illusion: trinkets, clothes, cars, material objects were inadequate. What Linus wanted could not be bought.

"Okay," he conceded. "Let's fight; let's see it through; let's sabotage the exam. But on one condition: I want to get Chem out of his prison." He looked away from the shopping center and walked back toward Mr. Zanz and Toscane, who were standing in the darkness, motionless and tongue-tied. "Did you hear me? We have to free Chem! That's all I ask. The organization needs him. He succeeded in switching our scores, in tricking the Great Processor. He'll know how to help us sabotage the exam. We can't let him—"

"It's impossible," Toscane said in a barely audible voice.

Mr. Zanz approached Linus slowly. Linus had a horrible premonition.

"Toscane is right," Mr. Zanz whispered. "A few weeks ago, Chem Nogoro's ID card was sent to the Administration of Persons. That's when I started being terribly frightened for you."

Toscane groaned. "Forgive me, Linus! I didn't know how to tell you. But it's true! Chem is dead too!"

Linus felt his strength drain out of him. He slumped to the floor. Toscane crouched down and took his hands in hers.

"I met Chem at the reeducation camp where I was doing my apprenticeship. I tried to help him but he did everything exactly as he pleased. One day, he managed to get into the computer monitoring area. He unlocked the alarm systems, the cell doors, the emergency exits, everything." She continued, half laughing, half crying, "He caused incredible chaos. If you'd only seen it! The freed students were running down the hallways, setting up barricades, wrecking equipment. No one, not even in Realm Three, had ever dared go that far." Her face darkened. "That night, a law enforcement unit put down the rebellion, and Chem was caught. He spent a week in an isolation cell. Then he disappeared. This was a few days before the end of my internship. When Mr. Zanz heard that Chem had been eliminated, he contacted me so I'd get you out as soon as possible. He feared for your life."

Mr. Zanz kneeled down next to Linus. "I'm sorry about Chem. Terribly sorry."

chapter 16

On Christmas Eve morning, Paris was under a blanket of snow. Overnight, white flurries had completely covered the streets, buildings, squares, and other landmarks. Icicles glistened under the branches of the trees bordering the deserted avenues. In the middle of the streets, the self-heating rails of the tramway looked like deep scars on the flawless layer of snow. Public transport wasn't operating at that early hour. Linus walked under the streetlights, his hands in his pockets. It had taken him more than two hours to reach the center of the city, and by now his feet were numb. *There's something to be said for anesthesia,* he thought, *for both physical pain and pains of the heart.* He kept on walking, unafraid, knowing his destination, like an arrow directed at a target. When Mr. Zanz and Toscane woke up, they would find his bed empty. And no note or explanation. Now that he knew they had hidden the truth from him about Chem, Linus no longer considered them trustworthy. Berthalia would tell them that she had seen him come down but that he hadn't told her where he was going. They would search high and low for him, but he would be miles away.

After a day spent locked in the hotel room in silent deliberation, he had settled on a course of action.

By the time he reached the neighborhood of the Ministries, Linus had noted signs of early morning activity. The windows of the buildings lit up, some shutters opened, and the electric wires of the tramway crackled as the system was turned on. He quickened his pace. Head lowered, nose buried in the scarf with the transit home colors, he thought about Chem. According to Mr. Zanz, Chem's ID card had been sent to the Administration of Persons a few weeks before. Though the idea seemed irrational, Chem's death coincided with the beginning of Linus's sore throat. Linus's glands had swelled as if his body had known what was happening.

As he walked by the entrance to a building, Linus screwed up his nose. The superintendent was hard at work in the lobby, near the incinerators, emptying the garbage into fireproof containers. The odor of burnt refuse seeped out of the building. On the opposite side of the street, the lights went on in one of the Zip entrances. Soon the whole city would awaken and activity would start up again. The workday would begin for thousands of people, amid order and indifference. Thousands of students would be going to their high schools, obsessed with the May exam, as he had been the year before.

Linus finally reached his destination. At the other end of a small snow-covered square was an ultramodern building with a rounded steel structure that looked like an upside-down Viking boat. On its facade was a silvery plaque with an engraved inscription: Administration of Persons.

Linus walked between the trees on the square and stopped near an old newsstand. Behind him, the first tram had just glided by noiselessly. Several sleepy pedestrians crossed the avenue, eyes downcast, carefully trying not to slip on the snow. Near the building entrance, Linus noticed a group of watchmen in a glass booth. He had to wait.

● ● ●

At eight o'clock, the first employees of the prestigious department entered the lobby and showed their ID cards. Squinting, Linus watched them from behind the newspaper stand.

He recognized a person rounding the corner of the square—his way of walking, his unusual appearance. Linus dashed toward him and called out as quietly as possible, "Yosh!"

Yosh stopped and his face lit up.

"Linus?" he said, stepping over a row of hoops running along the edge of a flower bed and joining him under the trees. "Boy, you really have a knack for showing up in the most dangerous places."

"I have no choice," Linus whispered. "Every place has become dangerous for me."

In his long winter coat of thermal fabric, Yosh looked disguised. He was wearing a Russian fur hat, which emphasized his strange moonlike face.

"I'm sorry I was so hard on you the other day," Linus

began. "I didn't expect to see you at my parents'. I didn't mean what I said."

Yosh shrugged. "Your grandmother said you had forgiven me. So let's drop it. Still, you had a narrow escape. You should have seen your father's face when the police came in to search the house. He almost had a heart attack! Two cops hung around the neighborhood for the whole weekend. They only stopped watching the house this morning. Tell me what I can do to help you."

"Get me inside," Linus said, pointing to the building with his chin.

Yosh gasped. "Are you crazy? They're searching for you far and wide!"

"I don't care. Get me in."

Yosh rocked from one foot to the other, indecisive and panicked.

"When you were living in Realm Two, you weren't so chicken," Linus said, egging him on. "Find a way of getting me past the checkpoint. It's very important!"

Yosh deliberated, perplexed, while scrutinizing the building facade.

"Get me a blank ID card," Linus insisted. "Your internship supervisor is a member of the organization. He'll help us."

"I know," Yosh mumbled. "But what about the cameras at the entrance? You're on file in the security system. It's too risky." His face and hands began to twitch as they always did when his nerves were on edge.

Linus grabbed him securely by the shoulders. He drew a deep breath and looked straight into Yosh's eyes. "Chem is dead," he said.

Yosh's tics stopped instantly. The blood drained from his face.

"Mr. Zanz has known this for several weeks," Linus said. "He confessed it to me two days ago. I want to understand what happened. You have to help me get my hands on Chem's confidential file."

Yosh opened his mouth but couldn't speak.

"Do it for his sake," Linus pleaded. "I'll wait for you here. Hurry up."

Yosh darted to the entrance, like someone driven by an invisible force. Linus watched him disappear inside, then hid behind the newsstand again.

Minutes went by; the sky over the roofs of the buildings began to whiten. Linus hopped up and down to keep warm. Time seemed to stretch out endlessly. On the newsstand windows he saw layers of tattered old posters. Very little was still legible: a few dates—2001, 2015—and the faded scarlet lettering of old magazine headlines referring to forgotten wars, assassinations, and retaliatory acts. He scratched off some frost with his fingernail. The world's forgotten memory had hardened there, on the shut-down newsstand. To recover it, he'd have to scratch a long time.

Suddenly he felt a presence near him, and he snapped out of his reverie.

"Slip this on!" Yosh said to him, trying to catch his

breath. He handed Linus a white cloth cap that would cover his head, neck, and upper shoulders. "I found an ID card for you in the name of Esteban Perez."

"Who is Esteban Perez?"

"A young guy who worked in the underground Industrial Zone. He survived a chemical accident . . . until this morning. We were supposed to receive him at two-thirty p.m. to reconfigure his identity, but he died overnight in the hospital. While the information is being processed by the computer center, you can be him. At two-thirty p.m. sharp, the computers will receive the order to delete his identity."

Linus slipped on the cloth cap.

"Don't say a word to the watchmen!" Yosh warned him. "Since your accident, you're unable to talk. Understand?"

"Yes."

Yosh handed him the ID card and led him to the entrance of the administration building. Immediately Linus started sweating under the cap covering his face.

The entrance to the lobby was blocked by an electronic gate. Yosh led Linus to the watchmen's cubicle and gave the door two short knocks.

"I was told to warn you that we've rescheduled an appointment for earlier," said Yosh.

"What's the person's name?" one of the watchmen asked, looking at Linus suspiciously.

"Esteban Perez," Yosh replied with composure. "He's got a second-degree burn on his face. He can't speak."

Linus swallowed and tried to keep calm. Would the

watchman believe this story? The man glanced at the computer screen. "He's down for a two-thirty p.m. appointment," he said.

"He has to go back to the hospital for a transplant," Yosh explained, unruffled. "That's why we had to reschedule his appointment."

"Do you have the order from the department head?"

Yosh showed the watchman a form. The watchman read it through the glass of the cubicle.

"Okay. Go ahead."

Yosh took Linus by the arm and led him to the electronic gate. "Your ID card," he whispered in Linus's ear.

Linus swiped the plastic square in the gate and heard a reassuring sound. Esteban Perez had the right to enter the sanctuary.

The two boys crossed the stately lobby without exchanging a word. A special kind of silence prevailed, rare and genteel—the kind of silence Realm One citizens were adept at surrounding themselves with. In spite of his anxiety, Linus noticed that his friend seemed completely at ease in the environment. *And what about me?* he asked himself with bitterness. *What have I become at this point?*

They went up two consecutive escalators, walked through a mezzanine, and entered a long, narrow room. Employees sat in transparent bubbles, working online. The walls of the room were lined with boxes holding thousands of digital discs. At the far end of the room, a door opened out onto a corridor with a row of doors to the managers' offices. Yosh knocked on the first door.

"I'm going to introduce you to Mr. Kandhour," he said. "He's the person who supplies Mr. Zanz with all the ID cards. And he's the one who came up with a way of getting you in."

Yosh pushed open the door for Linus. A very tall, unusually thin man rose from his armchair and extended his hand over his desk in a friendly manner.

"So? How are those burns?" he asked in jest.

Linus removed his cloth cap. "Thank you for your help," he said.

Mr. Kandhour bowed, with a hand on his chest. "I hope you find what you're looking for. Our administration is like a huge catalog. Everything is coded and archived here: deaths; births; marriages; genetic characteristics; medical, educational, financial, and political facts; plus records of each person's movements and trips. Yosh is an outstanding intern; he'll serve as your guide."

Linus turned to Yosh with a smile. "I knew that you were far from dumb!"

chapter 17

Later that morning, the two boys were enclosed in a soundproof bubble in the back of the archive room going over the contents of Chem's file. The coded data flashed by on the flat screen, and Yosh, a true virtuoso, translated the information for Linus.

"It's crazy!" Linus mumbled, his eyes riveted to the screen. "This machine knows everything there is to know about Chem's life."

Yosh pressed the touch screen with his index finger. "Look. Here are the medical bulletins put out by the hospital after his accident. And the police report on the fire."

Linus tried to concentrate on the digital codes, but they were like Chinese to him.

"Here are the documents of the verdict handed down by the Higher Court," Yosh explained. "And the sentence forbidding his parents to have another child."

Linus seethed with indignation. He knew that Chem's life had been far from joyful, but seeing these events posted crudely on a screen appalled him. He unbuttoned the top of his jumpsuit. Outside the bubble, employees were moving about, carrying discs to the genetics lab or boxes of paper archives to the shredders. According to

Mr. Kandhour, the department had almost finished coding the past three centuries' worth of old registers.

"I can't believe Chem is dead," Yosh murmured, shaking his head.

Linus put a hand on his shoulder. "I can't either. That's why I came. I want to see the data black on white."

Yosh focused on the screen again. "The problem is," he said as he continued reading, "some of the information is ultra-confidential. Permission is required. I discovered that confidentiality applies not only to criminal matters, but also to public personalities and large transfers of money—in short, to anything that's outside the norm. I came upon the same problem while trying to find traces of my brother's adoption."

"So you haven't located him yet?"

"Yes, I did, three days ago," Yosh said.

Linus started. "So? Where is he?"

Yosh sighed. "At the time my brother was born," he explained, "there was a massive campaign throughout the European Federation to encourage destitute Realm Two families to bring up only one child. The idea was promoted by a Realm One lobby consisting of sterile Realm One couples who wanted to adopt. They gave money to the parents."

"They bought babies?"

"Correct."

Linus was astounded. "Who purchased your brother?"

"A well-known guy," Yosh replied. "The man who designed the suburban shopping centers."

"Olf Bradman?" Linus said. "Are you telling me your brother is Olf Bradman's adopted son?"

Yosh nodded, his face expressing both helplessness and relief. Linus got up excitedly and told Yosh of his mother's connection with the Bradmans.

"Mom even had dinner at Bradman's house," he said. "She told me about his son. I mean . . . about your brother. But she didn't know, of course."

Looking deeply troubled, Yosh said, "Olf Bradman adopted my brother and gave him the name Seth. Seth Bradman." He smiled wryly. "Seth has lived like a prince all his life. Spacious house, good education, travel . . . The exact opposite of me, in other words." He waved away his gloomy thoughts with the back of his hand and said, "I'll deal with all that later. Let's get back to Chem."

Once again, the data flashed by and Linus understood none of it. With a worried look, Yosh opened the files, decoding and recording. Finally he stopped clicking and concentrated on a specific page.

"Here it is, the file on his internment in the reeducation camp. Well, Chem must have broken the rules several times. There are dates, length of time spent in solitary confinement, and, here, a note from the medical department."

Linus stared at the screen in an agony of sorrow. The day before, when Toscane had described the conditions under which Chem had lived, he had understood the meaning of the word "reeducation": a quasi military regime, beatings, punishments, insults, privations, and brainwashing sessions. Whenever Chem was out of line, he was sent to an isolation cell with no light or food. The camp was located in the mountains, at high altitude. At the first cold spell, Chem endured the worst abuse: he was thrown outside, barefoot, without even a T-shirt on his back, and had to spend the day running to survive the winter temperatures. It was hardly surprising to find the record of a medical visit. Anyone would have fallen ill under those circumstances.

Yosh leaned closer to the screen, intrigued by a sequence of numbers at the bottom of the file. "Not again!" he mumbled. "It's weird; these numbers don't correspond to anything. Yet this isn't the first time I've come across them."

Linus looked at the numbers without even trying to understand: 1.5.0. 03. 1.9.0. followed by several number signs. All of a sudden, Yosh struck the desk with his palm.

"I know where I've seen these numbers!" he shouted. "Exactly the same ones! This morning, when I explained your problem to Mr. Kandhour, he opened the files of the most recent ID cards we were sent. Among them was Dr. Ambrose's file and that's where I saw these numbers. I'm sure of it!"

Linus noticed that Yosh was having another attack of nervous tics. His left arm was moving uncontrollably. He got up from his seat and calmed himself by massaging his upper arm. The two boys exchanged lengthy, perplexed looks. What did this coded sequence mean? Linus closed his eyes, then leaned back in his chair to think.

"The only link between Chem and Dr. Ambrose is that they both knew Mr. Zanz," Linus said. Then something dawned on him. It was a mere intuition, a crazy idea. "Yosh, could you find the history of a Mrs. Flavitch?" he asked. "I don't know her first name. Her son is called Sadko."

● ● ●

At two o'clock, Linus and Yosh entered Mr. Kandhour's office. What they had just discovered was so strange they had no idea what to make of it. They had found the same numbers in Mrs. Flavitch's file, and in the files of all the organization members arrested on the day of the exam. In investigating more thoroughly, they had stumbled upon another detail that intrigued them.

"Did you find the information you were looking for?" Mr. Kandhour asked.

Yosh stepped closer to him. "Yes and no. Mainly, we have questions for you."

"Do you think it's possible to delete the digital data of a person who isn't dead?" Linus broke in.

Mr. Kandhour raised his eyebrows, surprised. He shook his head. "Here we don't delete anything. As long as a person is alive, his or her digital file is constantly updated. Once the person is dead, the information is archived and securely coded. No one touches it anymore."

"But what's the proof that a person is dead?" Linus asked.

"Well, the departments involved send us an ID card."

"Which departments?"

"Usually the local jurisdiction, hospital, or police headquarters. I don't think it's possible to delete anything. It would be too complicated."

Linus glanced at Yosh skeptically. "Yet in theory it would be possible?"

"In theory, yes," Mr. Kandhour admitted. "But it would be a serious act and completely illegal."

Yosh sighed. "When a person dies, they're buried or cremated, aren't they? And to close the file, the date and place of the ceremony are listed."

"That's right."

"What if this information isn't included in the file?"

Mr. Kandhour gave a start. "Impossible! If there's no indication of the burial place, then there's been a mistake, an oversight."

"So there's really something wrong," Linus replied. "We've found several such 'oversights.' "

Mr. Kandhour looked at him, flabbergasted. "How many files are involved?"

"About fifteen."

"And they're all members of the organization," Yosh added, placing a printout of the list of names on the desk. "What do you think this means?"

Mr. Kandhour picked up the list. He read through it rapidly, looking puzzled, furrowing his brow. "I have no idea what it means," he acknowledged. "We'd have to look into it."

Linus pointed to the list of names, which included

Chem's. "We think these people are alive," he said. "We have no proof; it's just a gut feeling but . . ."

"I'll look into it myself," Mr. Kandhour promised. "If your gut feeling turns out to be correct, I'll find a way of letting you know and of informing the heads of the organization."

"Thank you," Yosh said. "In the meantime could you give Linus a new blank ID card? Esteban Perez's won't be valid much longer."

Mr. Kandhour nodded and settled in front of his computer screen. "I won't leave your friend without an ID card for Christmas day."

Linus smiled. "Thank you for the gift."

"An ephemeral gift," Mr. Kandhour said apologetically. "Valid only twenty-four hours, as usual."

chapter 18

Once outside, Linus was relieved to remove his cloth
cap; then he smiled at Yosh and looked up at the sky. The
sun was like a pale disc behind the clouds, and the frozen
snow crunched under their feet as they walked to the Zip
station. Linus was in a daze. The supposition that Chem
might still be alive made him feel much better. It wasn't a
certainty, of course, but there was a glimmer of hope.
Why not believe in miracles? he thought. *It's Christmas
Eve, after all!*

"Don't you think we should contact Mr. Zanz?" Yosh
asked. "What we discovered may be really important."

Linus shook his head. "Mr. Kandhour will do it. We
had better limit our movements today."

"You're mad at him, aren't you?"

Linus raised his jacket collar and looked at his friend.
Yes, he was mad at Mr. Zanz.

"He didn't tell you the truth right away because he
didn't want to upset you," Yosh reasoned. "It isn't easy to
tell someone that their best friend is dead."

"That wasn't the only reason," Linus said. "Mr. Zanz
hid the truth from me because he was afraid I'd quit the

organization and stop cooperating. That's why I'm mad at him. He manipulated me."

"That's going too far!" Yosh protested. "Mr. Zanz isn't like that. He's been helping us from the beginning."

Linus shrugged. "He helps us as long as it benefits him. If I had known Chem was dead, I might not have agreed to escape from the transit home. He twisted my arm and made it impossible for me to back out."

"Maybe," Yosh said, "but what if Chem isn't dead?"

"If Chem isn't dead . . . that changes everything for me."

The two boys entered the Zip and went through the gate without a hitch. Linus held the cap in front of his nose to block out the stale vanilla odor in the passageways of the station and walked with his head lowered to avoid being filmed frontally by the cameras. Returning to the Protected Zone was risky, but he was determined to do it. There was no way he was going to spend Christmas all by himself, far from his family, like an abandoned dog. Also, on holidays the police usually concentrated surveillance on public places, such as department stores, theaters, and churches. He would be safer in the Protected Zone than in the Eldorado Complex.

When they sat down in the train, he leaned toward Yosh. "I'm dying to see their faces," he said with amusement.

Yosh sighed. "I just hope your father reacts well."

The stations flashed by; riders stepped in, stepped

out; the crowd thickened and thinned, depending on the stops. In the anonymous crowd, Linus felt almost secure.

"What about *your* parents?" he asked Yosh. "Aren't you going to visit them?"

"I'm going tomorrow. They have to work late tonight. It isn't like Realm One, where people set their own schedules. This is the first time in my life that I'm going to spend Christmas Eve with . . ." He hesitated to say the word. Linus said it for him.

"With family?"

Yosh smiled sadly. "Providing you're willing to lend me your sister and parents, of course."

"Were you always all alone before?"

"Not really. I had the TV." Yosh laughed. A second later his eyes misted over. "My dream is to spend next Christmas with my parents *and* my brother. All four of us together. But I doubt it'll be possible."

Linus didn't dare contradict him. But he knew that Yosh couldn't be more unlucky. He recalled what his mother had said about Seth Bradman: "He spoke like the head of a company, with self-confidence and contempt." There was a wide gap between Yosh and Seth. It was unlikely their meeting would be pleasant.

When they reached the end of the line, Linus and Yosh got off the train. They crossed the platform cautiously, making sure there was no police unit in the station. Everything seemed quiet. Yosh went through the security gate first, then signaled to Linus: the coast was clear.

Just as he was taking out his ID card, Linus heard hurried footsteps behind him. Next he felt a hand on his shoulder. His blood froze. He turned slowly. To his amazement, Berthalia stood before him, blushing with embarrassment.

"What—what are you doing here?" Linus stammered.

"Forgive me," Berthalia mumbled. "I followed you."

"You did? For how long?"

"Since this morning. And it hasn't exactly been a picnic. My feet are killing me, sweetie. You certainly gave me a run for my money."

Linus shook his head, flabbergasted.

"Mr. Zanz ordered me to keep my eyes peeled," Berthalia explained. "He suspected you might do something foolish. I wasn't supposed to let you out of my sight. Only now I can't go any farther. How can I cross into the Protected Zone with my Realm Two ID card? What am I going to say to Mr. Zanz? Oh dear, oh dear, he's going to be furious if I tell him I lost your trail!"

Linus rubbed his face nervously. He turned to Yosh, who was waiting impatiently on the other side of the gate and gestured to reassure him.

"Well?" Berthalia said insistently, wringing her hands.

"Tell him everything's fine," Linus whispered. "I'm spending Christmas Eve at home. Also, tell him that someone from the Administration of Persons is going to contact him concerning Chem and several other deceased people. If he has any information for me, let him come tomorrow at two-fifteen in the afternoon."

"To your house?"

"No. To the station, here."

"That's it?"

Linus thought for a moment. "No. Please send my love to Toscane. And wish her a merry Christmas for me."

Berthalia smiled and gave him a friendly tap on the back. "Merry Christmas to you too, honey bun."

Relieved that she no longer had to shadow him, she left Linus and went back to the platform to wait for the train.

"Who was that?" Yosh asked when Linus joined him on the other side of the gate.

Linus smiled enigmatically. "That was . . . the guardian of paradise."

They left the station. As they walked through the quiet streets, Linus tried to stop thinking about Mr. Zanz, Berthalia, and Toscane—and Sadko, who was most likely feeling sad tonight, all alone in the transit home. He tried to rekindle the excitement he had always felt in previous years as Christmas Eve approached, but he didn't succeed. He was frightened of seeing his father again. After all that time, would Mr. Hoppe still welcome him as his son? What if he rejected him?

When they arrived in front of the house, Linus paused. Standing on tiptoe, he saw the garden shrouded in mist and the house rising from the haze like an island in the middle of the sea. The lights in the living room shone in the dusk.

"Mieg must be back," Yosh whispered. "Do you want to warn her?"

"No, no. Let's just go in. Do you have the key?"

Yosh handed it to him. "Be my guest."

Trying not to tremble, Linus pressed the electronic release mechanism, and the gate opened. The light of the security system turned green. Still, Linus had a strange feeling, as if he were breaking into his home like a burglar. Yosh, very pale, had crossed his arms over his chest.

"You're not going to have a fit?" Linus asked anxiously.

"I'll try not to."

They had no sooner slipped into the foyer than they heard Mr. Hoppe call out from the second floor. "Francesca, is that you?"

"Darn," Yosh muttered, "your mother isn't home yet."

Linus felt his heart beat faster. Mr. Hoppe's voice was drawing nearer.

"You should call the caterer. He made a mistake with the order. He added an extra person . . ."

Mr. Hoppe appeared at the top of the stairs in sportswear, a towel hanging around his neck. He froze, gaping, his right leg suspended in midair. Linus looked up at him, trying to control his emotions and appear relaxed.

"Good evening, Dad."

Mr. Hoppe didn't move or speak. His eyes expressed astonishment and incomprehension. At that moment, Grandma burst into the foyer. Seeing Linus, she let out a cry and leaned on the wall to steady herself.

"I've come to spend Christmas Eve at home," Linus announced.

There was a protracted silence. Everyone remained rooted to their spots. It was as if the earth had stopped turning.

"Mieg is in her room. I'll go tell her," Grandma said, regaining her composure. She went up the stairs, and as she passed Mr. Hoppe, she whispered to him, "You should go kiss your son, Tobias."

"My son . . . ," Mr. Hoppe said foolishly.

Linus saw his grandmother disappear from the second-floor landing. The silence was so oppressive he felt as if there were no air in the room. For the briefest moment, he was tempted to run away.

Mr. Hoppe set his right foot down on the step and, clutching the banister, made his way down the stairs slowly. Linus noticed that the hair on his father's temples had turned white and that he had a worry wrinkle on his forehead. Aside from these details, his father hadn't really changed. But the long period of separation had created a gulf between them, and Linus suddenly felt intimidated. By the time Mr. Hoppe reached the bottom of the stairs, he was deathly pale. His towel dangled on his chest, and his breathing was impaired.

"Are you training for the Olympic Games?" Linus asked, forcing himself to smile.

"What?"

"Nothing."

Linus lowered his eyes, troubled and embarrassed. Yosh fidgeted next to him; he was having trouble controlling his tics. His head jerked up and down.

"I was going down to the basement," Mr. Hoppe announced, as though it were the most important news of the day. "I've set up a gym there."

Linus raised his eyes. He couldn't believe it. His father was going to work out.

"Oddly enough," Mr. Hoppe continued, "I don't have the slightest desire to lift weights anymore." He grabbed Linus and hugged him with all his might.

"Linus!" he cried out, whirling around the foyer like a madman. "You're back! You're home! Thank you! Oh, thank you!"

Clutching his father's shoulders, Linus felt giddy. They held each other tightly, overcome with emotion. Linus felt his heart swell and explode like a balloon. He burst into tears and so did his father. Linus saw Mieg and Grandma gaping at them from the top of the stairs.

The front door opened wide and Mrs. Hoppe appeared, muffled in her coat, holding a shopping basket.

"Francesca!" Mr. Hoppe shouted, rushing up to his wife. He seized her hand, closed the door, and led her to Linus. Mrs. Hoppe dropped her shopping basket.

"Linus has returned! He's going to celebrate Christmas Eve with us!" Mr. Hoppe announced.

Linus smiled at his mother. "I told you I'd be back home," he said.

While the three were hugging one another, Grandma and Mieg came downstairs. In the silence broken by sobs, Mieg went up to Yosh and put her hands gently on his shoulders. "I'm happy to see you both," she whispered. "But you might have been arrested. You're really crazy!"

Yosh turned his moon face toward her. "I know," he said, sighing. "But that's our charm, isn't it?"

chapter 19

A minute later, they were sitting in the living room.
Linus couldn't believe he was home, with his entire family, under one roof, just as before. He glanced at his mother, his father, his sister, his grandmother in turn and felt like a little boy returning home after a long vacation at summer camp. The objects in the room seemed both familiar and strange, almost unreal. Yosh sat apart, curled up at the far end of the couch.

"You took risks coming here, didn't you?" Mr. Hoppe asked finally. "The police searched the house last Saturday. They're looking for you. They refused to tell me why."

"I escaped from the transit home where I was locked up."

"Escaped?" Mr. Hoppe gasped. "Why on earth? Couldn't you just grin and bear it and wait for the end of the transition period? We could have come to see you in your foster family."

Mrs. Hoppe grasped her husband's knee firmly and signaled for him to let Linus speak.

"I was sick," Linus said. "And then, for reasons too complicated to get into, my friends felt it was urgent to get me out."

"Friends? What friends?" Mr. Hoppe asked.

Linus turned to Yosh, then to Mieg, looking for support.

Mieg stood up. "We can't tell you their names," she said. "Trust Linus, Dad."

Mr. Hoppe frowned. "Oh, because you're in on this too?"

He turned to his wife, then to Grandma, and suddenly his face turned red. "Don't tell me you're all in on it. Don't tell me I'm the only person in this house who didn't know what my son was up to."

"Tobias," Grandma said pleadingly. "Don't spoil everything!"

"So, please, fill me in, for heaven's sake!" Mr. Hoppe thundered. "Linus!"

Linus gave a start.

"Why hide everything from me? I've always trusted you. Ever since you were born, you and your sister, I've taught you to obey the rules and I've tried to make you into honest, law-abiding citizens. If there are no rules, society falls apart! You were admitted into Realm Two and sent to a transit home: fine, that's the rule. Now, without even blushing, you're telling me that you escaped? That you've become an outlaw, a deserter? How am I supposed to react?"

Grandma sprang up from the couch and stamped her foot. "You're right, Tobias! Society needs rules. But does that mean we have to accept any old rules? Can't you see how unfair the rules in our society are?"

"Oh, no, have pity!" Mieg pleaded. "You're not going to start arguing again."

"Be quiet!" Linus shouted. "Please be quiet!"

Instantly, they all fell silent.

"Hear me out without interrupting," Linus went on. His father's distress was painful to him. Linus owed him an explanation. "Promise?"

Overcoming his annoyance, Mr. Hoppe agreed to listen. He huddled in his chair, arms crossed, looking obstinate.

"The truth is I cheated on the exam," Linus began, not daring to look his father straight in the face. "With help from Yosh and Chem. We swapped scores. I did this because . . ." His voice cracked. He forced himself to look directly at his father before continuing. "Because I didn't want a ready-made future, ready for consumption, like a packet of soup. I know my future here wasn't bad. In a way it was even perfect. But it made me feel like I didn't exist. The life I was being offered wasn't really my life. Do you understand? I wanted to create my future myself, make my own decisions, find my own path. But with our exam system I realized I wouldn't be allowed to do this."

Mr. Hoppe remained stone-faced. Linus caught his breath and continued. "I met Yosh and, through him, other people who are fighting against the power of the Great Processor. There are many people who are unhappy living in pigeonholes with no chance of taking action or effecting change. It's thanks to them and Chem . . . and Mieg that I succeeded in getting into Realm Two."

Mr. Hoppe closed his eyes. He was obviously making an enormous effort not to explode with anger. In a controlled voice, he asked, "So now are you happy?"

"No," Linus replied. "I'm not happy."

"So you have regrets? You'd have preferred to stay in Realm One, is that it?"

Linus shook his head. "No, that's not it. I realized I wasn't comfortable either here or there." He glanced furtively at Yosh, who sank into the couch as if he wished he could disappear.

"The living conditions of Realm Two workers are awful," Linus went on, "and I don't think they're satisfied with them. I wish . . . I wish the realms didn't exist. I'd like to have the right to live with you but also close to Yosh and Chem. I'd like the arbitrary segregation of people to be abolished. I'd like to invent my own life without being in danger of being arrested by the police. I'd like to have the right to make mistakes, change my mind, make plans, and act on them." His chest shook with repressed sobs. "When I took the exam, I understood that there was no basis for the final calculations. How can a person be reduced to a score? It's absurd! The Great Processor is an illusion, a pretext for exerting power over people. Look at Yosh! His grade wouldn't have allowed him to live here, or to work at the Administration of Persons. Well, he's doing very well! The goal of the exam is to gag us and scare us; that's all. And those who are frightened submit to the law of the strongest. Do you think that's good—that the system exploits people's weaknesses?"

Mr. Hoppe gave a start, opened his mouth to reply, then changed his mind.

"My friend Chem was sent to Realm Three. Why? Because he openly criticized the system. And now he might be dead!"

Mieg looked as if she wanted to break in.

"It's not certain," Linus went on. "He was arrested by the law enforcement department and we've lost all digital trace of him. I can't help hoping he's still alive somewhere. But what I mean is it makes me sad to live in this kind of world. That's why I'm trying to do things differently. That's why I disobeyed."

Mr. Hoppe got up and went to the window. Linus followed him with his eyes. Linus's chin was trembling and he was struggling to hold back tears. Fortunately his mother came up to him.

"Your father needs time to reevaluate his beliefs," she whispered, taking his hand. "Give him time to think."

Linus nodded. Mr. Hoppe was visibly hurt and angry. Everything his son had just said went completely against his upbringing and Linus knew it.

After a while, with the silence dragging on, Grandma became impatient. "What about celebrating Christmas Eve? The caterer delivered the order. How about setting the table and warming up the dishes?"

No one replied. Mr. Hoppe left the window and walked over to the couch. "I meant to tell you," he said, surprisingly calm, "the caterer made a mistake. He delivered an extra serving of food." He turned to Linus, a hesitant smile on his lips, and added, "Quite a clever caterer, huh? Apparently he knew you were going to show up."

His heart thumping, Linus looked at his father and awaited his verdict like a criminal in court.

"I have no comment to make on what you did," Mr. Hoppe said. "I don't see the world the way you do, but I admit you had a lot of courage. There's one thing I do know, Linus: I want to celebrate Christmas with you— this Christmas and all the ones to come, if possible."

● ● ●

Fifteen minutes later, they were all seated at the dining room table. The strained atmosphere was gone; Mieg had put on some music, and delicious odors wafted in from the kitchen. On the white tablecloth, between the old-fashioned bottles of champagne, Grandma had set down candles and small baskets of exotic fruits. Mrs. Hoppe, her cheeks rosy from joy, burned her hands slightly as she served a dish of scallops.

"Here's to your first Christmas Eve without TV!" Linus said to Yosh as he poured a small amount of wine into his glass. Yosh smiled, but Linus could see that he wasn't really happy. He twisted the corner of his napkin nervously, probably preoccupied with thoughts of his own parents and brother.

Mieg leaned discreetly toward Linus. "It's been months since I've seen Mom look so cheerful," she whispered into his ear. "This is a terrific Christmas gift. But what are you going to do tomorrow?"

"I'll leave," Linus mumbled. "I have an appointment with Mr. Zanz at the station. He might have information for me about Chem."

"Then I'll come with you," Mieg said firmly.

Mr. Hoppe raised his glass, making the crystal tinkle. In spite of the wrinkle on his forehead, he seemed more relaxed. They all tried to pretend that this was a normal, cheerful, peaceful Christmas Eve like every other. But an uncomfortable feeling remained.

When everyone had been served, Yosh broke his silence. "I'd like to thank you for welcoming me into your home," he said. "You're all terrific people. I couldn't be luckier; that I know." He cleared his throat. "Linus explained why he wanted to swap with me. But I haven't told you *my* reasons."

The steaming scallops had been dished out, but no one dared touch them. Mr. Hoppe looked irritated, probably because he didn't know what other revelations were in store for him.

"Shortly before the exam, I found out I had a brother," Yosh said, still clutching his napkin. "He's a year younger than I am. He was adopted right after his birth by a Realm One couple that couldn't have children. Since then, I've been obsessed with one thing: finding him."

Everyone's attention was focused on Yosh. The flames from the candles shed flickering light on the faces around the table. Yosh continued in an increasingly hoarse voice.

"For months I've tried to track him down in the Administration of Persons' database. And finally I found him. His name is Seth. He was adopted by Olf Bradman."

Mrs. Hoppe stiffened and leaned toward Yosh. "Are you sure of this?" she asked.

"Absolutely."

Thunderstruck, Mrs. Hoppe nodded. "If what you say is true, I met your brother last year, shortly before the exam, when the Eldorado Complex opened. I had dinner at the Bradmans' to celebrate the opening."

"Linus mentioned it. What's he like?" Yosh asked faintly.

Mrs. Hoppe looked at him attentively. "Now that I think about it, Yosh," she said, "there's a slight physical resemblance between the two of you. Really, there is. Perhaps it's the hair. Yes, that's it; he has the same hair as you, and the same face shape. But with respect to everything else . . . I hate to tell you, but he was very unpleasant. Even disturbing. During dinner, he described the broad outlines of a project he had just implemented with his father's help. He boasted that he had a brilliant idea for making a particular category of delinquent fall back into line. According to him, it was a much more efficient system than the Realm Three reeducation camps."

Linus frowned. The first time his mother had spoken about Seth Bradman, he hadn't paid much attention, but that night an incredible thought flashed through his mind. "Did Seth go into his project in detail?" he asked his mother. "What kind of delinquents were involved?

Rebels? Computer hackers? Cybercriminals? Please try to remember!"

"I was only half listening," his mother said apologetically. "I can't tell you much more. With his superior smile and his businessman's vocabulary, Seth made me very uncomfortable. He seemed twenty years older than he is."

Yosh lowered his head and let go of his napkin. Linus had a feeling they were both thinking the same thing. Mr. Hoppe picked up his fork, having decided it was time to eat.

"Olf Bradman is a powerful manager," he said to Yosh between mouthfuls. "In the Economic Observatory's annual ranking, he's listed as one of the ten wealthiest men in the European Federation. It won't be easy for you to get into contact with that family."

Perplexed, Grandma and Mieg also picked up their forks and started eating the first course. Yosh and Linus, meanwhile, stared into space without moving.

"What if Seth's project—" Linus began pensively.

"Had something to do with Chem's disappearance?" Yosh broke in, finishing Linus's sentence.

The two boys looked at each other knowingly. It was a tentative hypothesis, but a plausible one. The Bradmans were powerful. Probably nothing seemed impossible to them. Not even deleting people's identities. Linus was determined to find out if there was a connection between them and the "dead" members of Mr. Zanz's organization.

chapter 20

On that freezing December 25, the streets in the Pro-
tected Zone seemed lifeless and dreary. A stormy sky
hung over the roofs of the houses, auguring snow. In the
foyer, Linus was buttoning up his jacket while his mother
looked on in dismay.

"Stay a few more days," she pleaded. "We can hide
you here. If the police come again, you can escape
through the garden. Why leave now?"

"There's someone I have to see," Linus said.

Since the previous evening, he hadn't stopped thinking about Chem and Seth Bradman. He and Yosh had sat
up talking about them most of the night. They had considered the link between Chem and Seth from every angle
and come up with a plausible set of assumptions: what if
Seth and his father had created a secret prison where they
detained special delinquents, such as Chem and Dr. Ambrose? By passing them off as deceased, they probably
avoided problems with the law. Of course, Linus and Yosh
couldn't be sure of anything. So they were impatient for
Mr. Zanz to tell them the information obtained by Mr.
Kandhour.

"After you've seen this person," Mrs. Hoppe said, "you'll come back home?"

"No, that won't be possible," Linus said. "My ID card is expiring in twenty minutes." He glanced into the living room to check the time on the plasma screen of the family computer. "Yosh!" he called out. "Hurry up!"

Yosh appeared at the top of the stairs with Mieg by his side.

"I'm going to the station with the two of you," she announced.

Linus responded to his sister's decision with a resigned sigh and turned to his mother. "I'm sorry I have to leave, Mom, but as long as I haven't found Chem, I'll feel awful."

Mrs. Hoppe nodded. "The house will always be open to you," she said softly. "Come back as soon as you can."

"I promise. Say goodbye to Grandma and Dad. They must have gone out and I don't have time to wait for them."

Yosh, Mieg, and Linus left the house quickly. Outside, a few snowflakes fluttered in the overcast sky. They walked briskly to the station without speaking.

When they reached the deserted Zip concourse, their footfalls echoed sinisterly under the tall vault of stone and metal.

"Are you sure Mr. Zanz will come?" Mieg asked, adjusting her hat.

"There's a train coming in two minutes. We'll see!"

"What if he doesn't show up?" Mieg asked.

"That would mean he has no new information about Chem and no explanation for the missing data in Chem's file. We'll have to keep looking."

Linus drew nearer to the translucent gate and scanned the platform. There wasn't a soul in sight. All the Realm One citizens were at home, savoring the happiness of their problem-free lives.

"Boy, you really spoke your mind last night," Mieg said. "Dad will have trouble recovering."

Linus sighed. "I didn't convince him, though, did I? It's too bad. I know he won't inform against me, or against Yosh either."

"I hope you never thought he could do that," Mieg said. "He loves you too much to ever do such a thing."

Just then, the noiseless train pulled into the station. Linus's heart pounded in his chest. From the gate, he saw several people get off the train and head for the concourse. Then he spotted Mr. Zanz and Toscane at the other end of the platform. He took out his ID card and turned to Yosh. "They're here. Are you coming?"

Just as he was about to swipe his card in the gate, he heard a voice calling out to him.

"Linus! Linus! Wait!"

He turned. His father and grandmother had burst into the concourse. They were running toward him, waving their arms.

"Wait!" his father repeated, catching up to him breathlessly. "We found something you might find interesting."

"It's about the Bradmans," Grandma said. "Your father and I have just been to the Economic Observatory."

Mr. Hoppe nodded nervously. "A quick round-trip! When your mother told us you had left, we ran all the way here!"

Linus didn't understand a thing. He glanced toward the platform. Mr. Zanz and Toscane were slowly approaching while the other riders filed past the gate and left the station.

"Listen, Linus!" Mr. Hoppe whispered. "I was tormented all night by what you told me at dinner. I had to check. This morning I found a computer trail of some of Olf Bradman's expenses."

"He deposited several million euros into his son's account," Grandma said.

"And Seth spends the money without a thought, using the name of a foundation," Mr. Hoppe said excitedly. "It's all rather shady. The money evaporates in complete secrecy. I think we're dealing with illicit operations."

Yosh yanked Linus's sleeve. Mr. Zanz and Toscane were waiting for them on the other side of the gate. Linus looked straight into his father's eyes.

"So you think I'm right? You think the Bradmans—"

"Perhaps!" Mr. Hoppe interrupted. "In any case, I'm going to tell the tax bureau to investigate their file."

Suddenly, Yosh let out a muffled gasp. "The police!"

Linus winced. A small group of men in uniform had materialized on the station platform and were charging toward the gate. Mr. Zanz and Toscane noticed them too late. Petrified, they didn't even attempt to run away. In a flash, the police were in front of them, demanding their ID cards. Linus, his eyes wide with terror, was incapable of moving. His father seized him violently by the arm.

"Follow me!" he said between clenched teeth. "The police won't check your identity if you're with me. You're on the good side."

Linus looked from Yosh to Mieg, then to his father and grandmother. The station clock showed 2:29 p.m. On the other side of the gate, without any raised voices, Mr. Zanz and Toscane allowed the men to surround them.

"I can't desert my friends," Linus said, his heart torn. He did some quick thinking. If he got himself arrested, he might follow the same route as Chem and the others. If he got himself arrested, there was a chance he could even find them.

"I'm sorry, Dad," he said to his father.

He shook himself free from his father's grasp, hurried to the gate, and swiped his ID card. The warning signal went off, as expected. "Invalid ID!" said the synthetic voice, and a flashing red light was set off. With the dexterity of predators, the policemen rushed over, unblocked the gate, grabbed Linus by the wrists, and snatched his ID card. Right behind him, Yosh leapt forward with a cry. He was intercepted. Just as the gate shut, Linus caught sight of his father's ashen face and Mieg looking at him uncomprehendingly, eyes filled with alarm.

chapter 21

Linus couldn't see a thing. A hood had been thrown over his head. He could only breathe through an opening near his nose. A cloth pad lay flat against his mouth, held by laces wound tightly behind his head. He couldn't even cry out anymore. He was inside a cold, echoing space that felt like the inside of a tin can. He tried to grasp something behind his back with his handcuffed hands, but found nothing. The can vibrated. From time to time he was jolted and rolled to the back of the can, bumping against a wall.

Mr. Zanz, Toscane, and Yosh were probably being subjected to the same treatment, but where were they? Linus felt as if he were suffocating under his hood. For long periods of time, he heard only the sound of his chaotic heartbeat. Earlier, at the station, the policemen had grabbed him by the nape of the neck. Then he had felt an electric discharge. He had lost consciousness and woke up in this space, all by himself, gagged, bound, and frightened.

"I chose to be arrested," he kept saying to himself, trying to silence his fears. "I could have listened to my father. I could have avoided being checked, but I chose to go through the gate."

The tin can stopped shaking. Linus managed to turn onto his back and sit up. With each breath he took, the fabric of the hood stuck to his nostrils. The coarse material smelled of dust and vomit. He swallowed painfully, but still felt nauseous.

And what if I'm wrong? he thought with dread. *What if Chem and the others are dead?*

Noises from the outside reached him; they sounded like shouts and screams. Then there was knocking on the wall. Linus turned his head from side to side in a futile attempt to understand what was happening. Sweat burned his forehead and trickled down between his eyes. He heard the sound of creaking metal.

"Get him out of there!" a voice commanded.

Linus gave a start. He felt hands lift him out of the can. Then he felt as if his head was being ripped off. It was only the rough cloth of the hood being pulled from his face. He started coughing. He couldn't breathe normally. But he could see and open his mouth once again.

In front of him were several police officers. With no word of explanation, one of them pushed him toward the entrance to a small room. Inside, Linus found Mr. Zanz and Toscane squeezed together on a bench, their hands attached behind their backs. They exchanged dread-filled looks. Linus sat down next to them in silence.

In the middle of the room, two men were checking something on a computer screen. Linus noticed three ID cards on the desk: his, Mr. Zanz's, and Toscane's. He wondered where Yosh's was.

No one said anything for a long time. Linus felt a tingling sensation at the nape of his neck. It felt stiff and he had trouble moving it. Mr. Zanz and Toscane seemed just as uncomfortable as he was. A pale light filtered into the room through a dirty windowpane reinforced with strong bars. The leather of the bench was cold and sticky. Linus wiggled, trying to stretch his bruised muscles.

Finally one of the two men stood up and came over to them. He had chubby hands and a freckled face.

"Your files are damning," he said. "You have no grounds on which to defend yourselves before the Higher Court. Prison sentences are inevitable, even for the two younger ones." He paused for a few seconds, then added, "But you still have a choice. If you wish, you can avoid being charged."

Linus turned toward Mr. Zanz slightly, his heart pounding: what did this offer mean?

"It's up to you," the man said. "But make up your minds fast." He looked as if he was about to leave.

Mr. Zanz called out to him. "Wait! Explain what you just said. How can we avoid the Higher Court?"

The man smiled and screwed up his eyes. "By accepting our offer of a compromise."

"What kind of compromise?"

"That's outside my area of responsibility. If this is the option you choose, I have to contact one of our partners. He'll explain the terms to you. I'll give you a few minutes to think about it."

He left the room. The other man was still absorbed in

his work on the screen. Linus swiveled around on the bench and looked at Mr. Zanz.

"We must avoid the Higher Court," Mr. Zanz whispered. "That's probably the option the others chose, before us."

"Did you find anything out?" Linus whispered.

"Yes, last night, from Kandhour. He checked and thinks you're right. Chem and the others aren't dead. Not physically, in any case."

Toscane leaned toward Linus, grimacing with pain from her stiff neck. "They're dead in computer terms," she said softly. "They've been deleted. But they must be somewhere, hidden away. That's what we came to tell you at the station."

Linus nodded. "So we should do the same thing. Accept their deal."

Mr. Zanz shut his eyes. "It's a big gamble. We have no idea what the compromise involves. It may be worse than prison."

Toscane and Linus stared at each other.

"That's possible," Linus said after a pause. "But if the others are still alive, I want to know."

Just then the man came back into the room. "So?" he asked. "What have you decided?"

"We'll accept the compromise," said Mr. Zanz.

"Fine." The man returned to the desk and started dictating coded commands into the computer mike.

"Where's Yosh?" Linus whispered. "I thought he was arrested too. I saw him dart toward us."

"They released him," Mr. Zanz whispered. "His ID card was valid."

Linus sighed. Of course, with his Realm One ID card, Yosh had the perfect right to be where he was, and the police had no grounds for arresting him.

The freckle-faced man put down his headphones and mike. "Go ahead! Take them away!" he ordered.

Three policemen burst into the room, brandishing electric clubs. Linus was brutally lifted, and before he had time to scream, he felt a new discharge burning the nape of his neck.

chapter 22

The first face Linus saw when he regained conscious-
ness seemed vaguely familiar. A man was looking at him
with a broad, phony smile, his fleshy lips spread over a
row of perfectly aligned white teeth. Linus blinked. The
nape of his neck hurt. He tried to recall where he had seen
this man and suddenly he knew: on the giant screen
above the Eldorado Complex dome. He even remembered
the flashing slogan under the image: Olf Bradman,
founder of the shopping center, wishes you a bargain-
filled day!

However, this was not a photo. Olf Bradman was
standing before him, in the flesh, his paunch sticking
out. From the smug look on his face, it was clear to Linus
that Bradman was the one who had just negotiated a
bargain.

"I'm sincerely sorry for the bad treatment you received," Olf Bradman said. "The police use methods I dis-
approve of. But now it's over. Can I offer you anything to
drink?"

Linus managed to sit up. His head felt as if it weighed
ten tons. Dazed, he noticed that he was sitting on a couch,
in a comfortable oval living room. His handcuffs had been

removed. Not far away, Mr. Zanz and Toscane were coming out of a daze too.

"Lemonade?" Olf Bradman asked. He handed Linus a glass.

"You've made a wise decision," he said. "I congratulate you. With your checkered pasts, the Higher Court would have given you a harsh sentence. And unfortunately, the public prisons in this country are dens of despair and iniquity." He sighed. "What a waste; don't you agree? All this brilliant youth, these wasted intellects! I'm appalled they put people of your caliber in prison. Fortunately, we've found a way of bypassing the Higher Court."

Linus looked at the liquid in his glass. He was very thirsty but suspicious, and he preferred not to drink. He glanced at Mr. Zanz and Toscane; they were sitting very still, listening to Bradman's speech.

"I'm sure you wonder how such an arrangement is possible," Olf Bradman resumed, smiling. "Yet, with a lot of money and some helpful connections, it's a cinch. The Bradman Foundation has an agreement with the police and they send us the delinquents they've arrested. I don't mean thieves or criminals! They can rot in hell. I mean far more interesting delinquents: people like you, who have attacked the system, rebelled against the established order, and tried to interfere with the way society works." Bradman swallowed a whole glass of lemonade in one gulp and then declared, "I'm intensely interested in people like you. And do you know why? Because you've succeeded in outwitting the law! An accomplishment that required unusual and valuable qualities: energy, determination, intelligence, speed, flexibility, creativity, courage." Carried away, Bradman poured himself another glass. "I admire you!" he went on. "And yet one thing bothers me." He came closer to Linus and stared straight at him with his pale icelike gaze. "What bothers me is you're my enemy!" Bradman said contemptuously. "You've declared war on the system that serves my interests. And I have no intention of putting up with that."

Linus was now wide awake. With a feeling of oppression in his chest, he concentrated on Bradman's words and tried to figure out what he was driving at. Bradman had moved close to Mr. Zanz. He pointed his finger menacingly. "You underestimated the enemy, Zanz! Your organization wasn't up to it. Now I've caught you. Officially, you people don't exist anymore. Your ID cards have been sent to the Administration of Persons and you're considered dead."

Linus tried to control a shudder. He felt as if he were in the heart of a labyrinth, right in the Minotaur's den. Here was the monster, so close to him he could touch it. But if he wanted to knock it down, he would have to wait. He would have to understand it and gauge its strength.

"However," Bradman resumed, flashing his phony smile again, "as you may have noticed, you're not dead. I'm offering you life . . . and many other things as well. We merely have to come to an agreement, you and I."

Mr. Zanz rose from the couch, looking very tense. Drops of perspiration stood out on his balding brow.

"Who exactly are you, Mr. Bradman? What do you expect from us?"

"Don't be so distrustful, Zanz," Bradman said. "Actually this was my son's idea. A brilliant idea: our foundation buys delinquents, rebels of your ilk, and recycles them like old paper. Don't get offended; many pretty, very interesting things are made with old paper. My son will give you a detailed explanation." He walked rapidly to a door at the other end of the room.

"And what if we reject your agreement?" Mr. Zanz called out.

Bradman turned, surprised. "No one has rejected it yet!" He clapped his hands, and the door opened. "Let me introduce my son, Seth. He'll know how to convince you."

Bradman slipped out, turning things over to Seth, who strode in nonchalantly. The door closed behind him. Upon seeing Seth's face, Linus stifled a cry of surprise. His resemblance to Yosh was striking: the same flat face, the same overly large eyes, the same hopelessly unruly hair. Only his composed demeanor and well-fed adolescent build made him unlike his brother. He stopped in the middle of the room and took his hands out of his pockets. Without saying a word, he held out his arms and opened his palms. Troubled by Seth's uncannily familiar demeanor, Linus didn't immediately notice what Seth was showing them.

"Do you know what I have here?" Seth asked calmly.

Linus looked at Seth's hands. In the middle of each palm he saw something small and black.

"These are implants," Seth explained. "Little electronic devices that have been inserted under my skin. It's a delicate operation, but risk-free."

Linus felt nauseous. From the corner of his eye, he saw that Mr. Zanz and Toscane were just as dismayed as he.

"These implants are much more convenient than digital ID cards," Seth continued. "In time, they will replace cards, but for now only a small number of us are equipped with them." He smiled, and Linus noticed that the boy bared his teeth in the same phony way as his adoptive father did.

"With these implants, you couldn't have used the blank ID cards you had. This new branding technique makes cheating impossible. Unless you cut off your hands."

He spoke the words with cold detachment. Linus began to understand why his mother had found Seth so disturbing.

With a satisfied chuckle, Seth put his hands back into his pockets and crouched down in front of Linus. "I know someone who would like to see you, Linus. He was arrested a few weeks ago, after we were informed of his acts of bravery in a Realm Three camp. A very, very brilliant mind."

Linus felt himself go pale. He couldn't refrain from mumbling, "Chem? Chem is here?"

"Of course he's here. Do you want to see him?"

Linus nodded. In spite of his revulsion toward Seth, he felt happy and relieved. His hypotheses were confirmed: Chem was alive and Linus would be seeing him soon.

Seth smiled, screwing up his eyes. "Patience. As soon as you and I have come to an agreement, you'll see your friend."

"What agreement?" Linus asked.

Seth took his hands out of his pockets again and held them out so that Linus could take another look at the implants. Each one was a small shiny black disc, a small bulge in the hollow of the palm.

"The agreement is simple. We offer you a safe life and whatever your heart desires. In exchange, you agree to wear implants like these and to work for our foundation."

Linus felt cold sweat run down his back. He stared at Seth's palms with disgust. That kind of thing embedded in his skin seemed far worse than the tracking bracelet the director of the home had clasped around his wrist on the night he had escaped.

"Whatever your heart desires, Linus," Seth said again, seeing him hesitate. "And I'll keep my word. Think hard. What's your deepest wish?" Since Linus didn't answer, Seth turned to Toscane. "You too can have whatever your heart desires if you agree to wear these little implants and help us out."

Toscane, who hadn't said anything for a long while, looked at Linus with her dark eyes. They were full of distress. He sensed her inner turmoil, her deep anger mixed with weariness and surrender. Then he saw two tears appear and roll down her round cheeks.

"It's all over," she murmured. "We've been had."

Linus felt his throat tighten. Toscane's emotion devastated him. He got up and went to sit next to her.

"You're going to accept; I know you will," Toscane said. "You'll accept their offer because you want to see Chem again. And I'll imitate you so that I can stay with you—with all of you—because you're the only family I have. That's how they trap us, Linus."

Seth stood up, visibly amused by Toscane's words. "She's perfectly right! All the people we've arrested up to now have had the same reaction. They've accepted the offer because it's in their interest. Your friend Chem will tell you: he's happy with his fate. We gave him what his heart desired. To begin with, we gave him freedom. No more reeducation camp, no more violence, no more confinement. But most important, we got the Higher Court to revoke its sentence. Chem's parents are now allowed to have another child. Thanks to us, and because he showed himself to be reasonable, Chem will probably have the immense happiness of having brothers and sisters."

Dumbfounded, Linus leaned back on the couch. If the Bradman Foundation could manipulate the police, the courts, the identity of people, then it could surely obtain anything. He looked at Seth and, without thinking, blurted out, "What do you know about the happiness of having brothers and sisters? You have a brother and you don't even know him."

Seth crossed his arms and leaned forward slightly, a sly smile on his lips. "You mean Yosh?"

Linus jumped up, electrified. "You know about Yosh?"

"Of course. My parents never hid from me that I was adopted. They're not dumb—unlike my biological parents. I've always known that I had a brother. A stupid kid, in fact. I was very surprised he was admitted into Realm One. But never mind! I've never wanted to meet him. He can stay where he is. I'll be none the worse for it."

Linus was transfixed, speechless from anger and incomprehension, while Toscane became extremely agitated.

"Yosh is Seth Bradman's brother?" she asked, stunned.

Linus nodded and turned to Mr. Zanz, who was slumped in a chair and shook his head with distress and helplessness.

"Yosh discovered the identity of his brother only a few days ago," Linus said. "This adoption story was his special secret. I wasn't supposed to talk about it."

He straightened his back and looked Seth up and down. "His only wish has been to find you. He'd love to talk to you. But if I have the opportunity, I'll tell him not to bother. Yosh is a hundred times better than you. He isn't stupid! He's only been raised in difficult circumstances. However, thinking about it, I wonder if he wasn't luckier than you!"

Seth burst out laughing. "You know what the difference is between you and me, Linus?" he said. "You get attached to people. This is a major weakness; it will always prevent you from fully profiting from life." He suddenly became gloomy. "Enough chatter. We're offering you what you want: freedom; your friend Chem, whom you miss so much; the eradication of your police record; and peace of mind for your family. So, do you accept or not?"

Linus began to tremble. He tried to catch Mr. Zanz's eye, but the resistance organizer sat motionless, his head in his hands.

"And what if I refuse?" Linus asked weakly.

"If you refuse, we'll arrange to have your parents and sister arrested. However, they won't be as lucky as you. Since our foundation isn't interested in them, they won't be given a choice; they'll be sent directly to prison. It's up to you."

Mr. Zanz got up and went over to Linus. An uncertain glow flickered in his green eyes, but his voice was perfectly clear. "Accept. It's the only solution," he said softly.

chapter 23

Two days later, Linus opened his eyes and saw that he was in a hospital room, lying on a bed with wheels, his arms strapped down and his hands bandaged. Just as he was regaining consciousness, a door opened and an unfamiliar woman entered. She was wearing a nurse's uniform.

"Don't try to move," she advised. "I'll warn the doctor that you're waking up."

She left, and a few minutes later, another woman came. Linus's heart skipped a beat as he recognized her.

"Dr. Ambrose?"

She walked up to his bed. "I'm happy to see you alive, Linus," she said softly. "How do you feel?"

He swallowed with difficulty. "I'm thirsty."

"That's normal. It's the effect of the anesthetic. But you'll have to wait; you shouldn't drink anything for another few hours."

Linus closed his eyes and tried to recall what had happened. The last thing he remembered was agreeing to Seth Bradman's offer and being taken to a lab, where he'd undergone a series of medical tests. He raised his head, gazed at his bandaged hands, then looked at Dr. Ambrose.

"Was it you who put in the implants?"

She nodded and pulled up a chair next to the bed. "This is what I do for the Bradman Foundation. In exchange, they leave my family alone and allow me to engage in high-level medical research." She sighed. "That's life, Linus. Sometimes you have to face reality and give up some dreams. I operated on Toscane too. She's waking up in the room next door."

Linus licked his dry lips. "What about Mr. Zanz?"

The question seemed to upset the doctor. "By the way, you have a visitor," she said, changing the subject. "Since you're all right, I'll come back later."

Linus knitted his brows as he watched her leave. A few seconds after, he saw a head pop through the doorway. He couldn't even cry out; emotion made him tongue-tied. Then Chem appeared in his entirety.

"Greetings, Cookie!" he called out joyfully.

Chem's tall body, wide shoulders, and big laugh instantly warmed Linus's heart. He was whisked back to the past, to the time when the two of them had been ordinary students who spent their recreation period planning to refashion the world. A wave of nostalgia made him smile.

"Dr. Ambrose left your straps on?" Chem said with surprise. He came to the bed and untied them.

"There." He smiled. "You're free, Cookie!"

Cookie! How many times over the years had he begged Chem not to call him that? But now he wasn't complaining; he was thrilled to hear that silly nickname. Sitting up in bed, he rubbed his sore arms but didn't take his eyes off Chem.

"So? Have I changed?" Chem asked him.

"A bit," Linus admitted.

"With what I went through in Realm Three, I built up my muscles. Look!" Chem rolled up the sleeves of his jumpsuit and flexed his biceps with amusement.

"You've always been a big strong guy." Linus laughed. "No, you've changed in some other way."

Chem sat down in a chair, looking happy. Linus scrutinized him. His eyes settled on his friend's neck.

"Your scarves," he said. "You're not wearing your scarves!"

"Bingo! And do you know why, pinhead?"

"Your scars are hardly visible."

Chem raised his chin proudly so that Linus could admire his nearly smooth neck, minus the pale puffy scars that used to make him so self-conscious.

"A new plastic surgery technique!" Chem cried out. "Dr. Ambrose performed it on me when she put in the implants."

He turned his palms toward Linus. A small shiny black disc was embedded in the middle of each palm.

"It looks weird," said Linus.

He looked at his own hands. He knew he would find the same thing under the bandages, a prospect that made him grimace. "We were trapped like fools, weren't we?" he said. "What are they asking you to do in exchange for all this?"

Chem leaned close to him with a confidential air. "I'm working on various computer programs," he whispered. "The foundation gave me the assignment of optimizing their monitoring system. It's very interesting." He leaned back and winked at Linus cheerfully. "Don't get discouraged, Cookie. They bought us as if we were merchandise, but we're not merchandise, right?"

Linus nodded. After the intense joy of their reunion, he suddenly felt overwhelmed with sadness.

"Yosh and Mieg were with me when I was arrested. They'll try to find us, but . . ."

Chem sighed. "They could be looking a long time, I'm afraid."

"We were on Bradman's trail," Linus explained. "We had examined the information and put it all together and come to the conclusion that you were alive. I'm sure Yosh won't believe that we're dead. And Seth promised me I'd be free. If I can move around, I'll find a way of seeing my parents."

Chem shook his head sadly and pointed to his implants. "They promised me I'd be free too, Cookie. But having these things under your skin is like being in a cage. Believe me, if I'd been free, I'd have tried to find you too." He poked one of the black devices with his fingertip. "I walked out of here one day and didn't get beyond a hundred yards."

Linus opened his eyes wide, alarmed. "Why?"

"As soon as you try to go through a gate or get within range of a detection terminal, you receive a powerful electrical charge. It makes you feel as if you're going to die. I collapsed from the pain. I'm not about to try again."

Linus looked at his bandages in despair. "I don't understand," he said. "Seth himself has implants."

"They're not the same kind as ours. Seth can go

through whatever gate he wants. He had them implanted because he enjoys provoking people."

"So they lied."

"No, they didn't," Chem said. "In theory we're free. We can go out. No one is preventing us. The only watchmen are right here, in our hands. The pain is unbearable. There are detectors everywhere: in the Zip gates, in the doors of shops, in houses, in trams, you name it. This is the only place where we're safe."

"Here?" Linus said, panicked. "In this hospital?"

"We're not in a hospital, Cookie. We're . . ." Chem trailed off, then asked, "Can you get up? Come and look out the window."

With effort, Linus got to his feet and let himself be guided to the window. Chem raised the shade and Linus stood on tiptoe. A dizzying hundred yards below he saw a large rain-drenched esplanade that he immediately recognized.

"The exam center?" he said.

"Right. The Bradmans set up their foundation in the skyscraper overlooking the center. They have thirty stories all to themselves."

He lowered the shade and looked at Linus. "Now we know who's behind the Great Processor: the Bradman Foundation. It's headed by a small group of powerful managers—the same people who devised the exam system and the different zones years ago. They work here, in this skyscraper, and form a kind of exclusive micro-realm. They call it Realm Zero. And now we're at their mercy. It's the height of cynicism, isn't it? We're working directly for the Great Processor, Cookie."

Linus closed his eyes. He felt like stopping up his ears and howling with rage. But Chem put his large hand on Linus's shoulder.

"Hey!" he whispered. "We're together, aren't we? Let's not give up hope. You and I have already accomplished great things."

Linus breathed deeply. "What about Mr. Zanz?"

"Come sit down," Chem whispered.

Linus looked at him, distraught; feeling his legs go weak, he willingly went back to the bed.

"The truth is Mr. Zanz rejected their offer," Chem said, his voice trembling. "He waited until Toscane and you were out of the room, and then he turned it down outright. I think they eliminated him immediately afterward." He sighed in sadness. "This time, they weren't bluffing. Dr. Ambrose saw his corpse. Mr. Zanz really is dead, Linus."

The blood drained out of Linus's face. He felt faint and could barely make out the rest of what Chem was saying. "We're at the heart of the system," Chem continued. "It's an opportunity for us. I've already thought about what to do."

Linus nodded, but was unable to speak.

"The next exam is in five months," Chem whispered. "If we're cautious, if we play along with them and obey the foundation rules, we might be able to sabotage everything. Mr. Zanz would be proud of us, wouldn't he?"

chapter 24

The following morning, Linus and Toscane were allowed to leave the hospital unit. A closemouthed foundation employee took them to the twenty-third floor of the building. Seth was waiting for them.

"Welcome to the Bradman Foundation Research Center," he said, leaning against a reinforced door with a smile on his face. "This is where you're going to work." Like a butler at the entrance to a mansion, he stepped aside and extended his arm to let Toscane pass. "Ladies first."

She hesitated, then walked up to the door. There was no doorknob, no lock, no latch with which to open it.

Seth sniggered. "Sorry, I forgot to tell you that to be admitted into the high-security labs, you have to place your hand on the genetic decoder." He pointed to a smooth dark plate next to the door. Toscane threw a sideward glance at Linus, then put her left hand on the plate. Nothing happened.

"You have to press harder," Seth instructed her.

Toscane obeyed, then stiffened and cried out in pain. Linus rushed to her side. She had jumped backward. A red mark, like a burn, was spread over her palm.

"Oh, I'm sorry," Seth said. "I forgot! Your implants won't let you in." The smile vanished from his face as he placed his own hand on the genetic decoder. The reinforced door opened immediately.

"Filthy dog!" Toscane grunted. "He did it on purpose."

Linus gave Seth a withering look, but he had already walked on, laughing to himself.

"Of course I did it on purpose," Seth said. "That little experience seemed essential to me. That's the only way to deal with people like you. The tough method is all you understand."

Linus held Toscane by the shoulders, and together they crossed the threshold. Seth strode ahead of them, into a room filled with computer hardware, and began explaining things in a pompous tone.

"This lab was designed according to my specifications. It has unusually powerful computing capacity. The software in all these terminals is upgraded on a daily basis, thanks to your friend Chem's valuable collaboration." He stopped in front of a long table with rounded edges and ran his fingertips over the surface. Two flat screens popped up in the center of the table.

"Your workstations," he said. "This is where you'll be coming every day. Go ahead, sit down." He pointed to two plastic hulls that included seats, but Linus and Toscane remained standing, looking defiant and obstinate. "As you wish." Seth sighed. "But let me explain my plan. It's simple yet . . . brilliant." A big smile lit up his face. Linus clenched his teeth as an uncontrollable feeling of resentment welled up in him.

"You're antiestablishment rebels," Seth continued. "Instead of preventing you from taking action, I've decided to make you into retrievers. Now that you've signed an agreement with the foundation, you've become our hunting hounds." He tapped a screen lightly. "The prey is in here, in those files. You're in charge of chasing it, trailing it, and bringing it to your master."

Linus stared at the screen uncomprehendingly.

"You'll have access to the files of all the examinees," Seth explained. "Even the most confidential information. You'll study the cases one by one: school records, health records, bank records, family records, club memberships, etcetera. You'll go over everything with a fine-tooth comb, analyze and classify the data, and establish the students' psychological profiles." He leaned close to Linus's ear. "Except mine, of course." Linus gave a start. He looked hard at Seth, who went on. "Your work will consist of spotting students who have a profile similar to yours: i.e., the rebels. It takes one to know one, right?"

"I thought the Great Processor detected them," Linus said.

Seth looked at him with contempt. "The Great Processor is none of your business. If you refuse to do this work, we'll have your parents arrested. Is that clear?" He turned to Toscane. "As for you, if you don't cooperate, we'll take it out on your mother."

"My mother?" Toscane said. "But . . . she's dead!"

Seth crossed his arms over his chest. "We know she's dead. In fact, she was a respectable person; may she rest in peace. But you see, we could tarnish her reputation—by revealing her affiliation with a terrorist network, for example."

Toscane turned pale. "My mother wasn't a terrorist!"

"That's just one possibility," Seth replied. "We'll have no trouble coming up with other ideas, things that are even more dishonorable. You know the law: her coffin would be removed from the cemetery and destroyed."

Linus saw the desperate expression on Toscane's face. Without thinking, he pounced on Seth and grabbed him by the collar of his jumpsuit. They exchanged looks, but Seth remained impassive.

"You should learn to control yourself," Seth said calmly. "Don't forget: our side has the power."

Reluctantly, Linus released his hold.

"Good. I think we've understood each other. Now get to work. Your job is to provide us with at least three student names a week. After that, our surveillance and law enforcement units will take over."

Linus and Toscane heard the reinforced door open again and saw a group of people enter the lab.

"Oh, here are your colleagues," Seth announced. "I'm sure you'll recognize some of them. They were all members of Zanz's organization." He went to the other end of the room, a smug, self-satisfied look on his face.

Among the newly arrived Linus noticed a tall, thin woman with light blond hair who bore a striking resemblance to Sadko. She followed the flow calmly and sat down at her computer terminal. The lab suddenly started buzzing like a beehive, keyboards clicking. The rebels, the dissenters, were slaves now, working for their enemy.

Linus turned to Toscane with a lump in his throat. The alarm in her eyes made him want to console her. Instead he leaned toward her and whispered, "Courage! Chem will come up with some way to get us out of this mess!"

In midafternoon, Linus and Toscane left their work-
stations. An employee took them to their rooms on the top
floor of the skyscraper.

The foundation hadn't skimped: they were each given
a spacious, comfortable, light-filled room with an attached bathroom including an exercise and relaxation
area. Linus noticed a bouquet of fresh flowers on a
pedestal table, and a built-in beverage machine. At the
foot of his bed, he found a metal cabinet containing a
complete video set providing voice-activated access to a
full range of entertainment. Just then, there was a knock
at the door and Chem came in.

"Have you checked out that beauty?" Linus asked,
pointing to the video set.

"It's an experimental model, not on the market yet,"
Chem said. "But don't bother looking for a computer or
anything resembling a telephone line. The only place
you'll find those is in the high-security labs on the lower
floors."

Disappointed, Linus shut the cabinet. "By the way, I
didn't see you downstairs. Don't you work in the lab?"

"Special treatment for geniuses, Cookie!" Chem said.

"I'm entitled to a special office on another floor. You should see it: a pure technological marvel."

Linus glanced at him with bitterness. "It almost seems as if you enjoy living here."

Chem chuckled. "Me? Of course I enjoy it. Look at all this luxury! The foundation also provides us with food and clothing. What more could anyone desire?"

Linus trudged to the bathroom, fiddled with the light dimmer for a few seconds, then came back and said, "I don't know about 'anyone.' But Mr. Zanz is dead. I'm separated from my parents again. I have to inform against innocent kids, and I have to put up with Seth's constant threats. So I couldn't care less about the luxury."

Chem shrugged. "It depends on how you see things. I spent months in a reeducation camp, with ten days in solitary, in total darkness, sleeping on the cold damp floor, so I'm not about to bite the hand that feeds me."

Linus collapsed on the bed and heaved a deep sigh. He looked at his hands and grimaced. "I'll never get used to these implants under my skin," he said.

Toscane entered the room. Linus noted that she had changed clothes and taken the trouble to put her hair up in a bun. She shut the door behind her and went up to Chem.

"I inspected my room thoroughly. I didn't find a single mike or camera. Does that mean we're not under surveillance?"

Chem opened his palm. "The implants are all they

need. As a result, we can speak freely in the rooms . . . and play on these consoles. How about a little game?"

He kneeled down next to the metal cabinet while Linus lifted his eyes to the ceiling. He couldn't believe how insensitive and immature Chem was acting. How could he think of playing video games when their situation was so desperate?

Chem opened the cabinet, pulled the audio-video player out of its case, and gestured for Linus to come closer. "I'm suggesting a very special game," he whispered. "Look, each room has the same type of equipment. It operates on a closed circuit, but by fiddling around a bit . . ."

Chem smiled, winked at Linus, and started to unplug the cables to examine them. Linus felt his heartbeat quicken. He knew Chem so well he sensed his excitement from the slight trembling in his voice. It was an unmistakable sign: the computer genius was at work.

"I have to assemble the parts from these different units," Chem explained. "I'll find everything I need in them: optical cables, digital cards, plasma monitors, and more." He fell silent, deep in thought. "I've been mulling this over for several weeks," he finally continued. "If I have a sufficient number of optical fibers and put together a router and a powerful enough connection adapter . . ."

A shiver ran down Linus's spine. "You're going to cobble together an illegal computer?" he asked.

Chem put a finger to his lips. "Yes," he said in a very low voice. "A true war machine. But I'll need your help."

Linus no longer knew what to think; his mood fluctuated between hope and despair. Toscane sat down on the bed. Out of the corner of his eye, Linus saw her wringing her hands nervously.

"Tell me what we have to do," Linus whispered after a long pause.

"We have to dismantle each set," Chem explained. "We'll proceed in stages and in absolute secrecy. I'll ask you for specific parts; we'll find some way of getting them to me. I'll connect the parts inside my own set, in my room. If I work every night, I should succeed."

Toscane cracked her knuckles.

"I even managed to steal a few tools," Chem went on. "My desk looks like a supermarket." He turned his pockets inside out and showed them a screwdriver, a microscopic soldering iron, and pliers for stripping the cables.

"That's risky," Linus said. "If they notice missing tools, they'll search our rooms."

"Don't worry, Cookie! I'll put them back where they belong every morning."

"And then what?" Toscane asked. "What will you use this illegal computer for?"

"My plan," Chem said, "is to get inside the Great Processor's memory. If I can do that before the exam, all I'll have left to do is design a parallel program to replace the official one." He turned to Linus, and added, "Your score swap with Yosh was only a trial run. This time around we'll do things on a grand scale."

Linus saw a glimmer in Chem's eye and suddenly grasped what he wanted to do. In a faltering voice, he asked, "You mean you could program an exam-wide swap of all the scores?"

Chem began to laugh softly. "Can you imagine the chaos? Not one examinee admitted into his original realm. Thousands of downgraded students. Thousands of families faced with the absurdity of the system. That would guarantee a revolution!"

Linus and Chem smiled at each other. It was a dangerous, insane idea, but it seemed like the obvious thing to do.

"We have to stick it out for another five months," Chem added, his tone becoming serious again. "In the meantime we'll have to play along with the Bradmans. The fewer suspicions they have, the more they'll let me work in peace."

Linus and Toscane exchanged looks.

"No problem for me," Toscane declared. "I'm used to passing myself off as an obedient child."

Linus put his hand on Chem's shoulder. He felt his heart beat with excitement. "Your little game appeals to me," he said. "When do we start?"

chapter 26

Weeks went by. Life in the skyscraper was regulated like clockwork. During the day, everyone worked for the foundation, and Linus obeyed Seth's orders conscientiously so he wouldn't suspect anything. Olf Bradman frequently dropped in on the research lab. He strode around the computers, hands in his pockets and paunch sticking out, beaming with pride. Just by the expression on Bradman's face, Linus assumed that nothing was interfering with the even course of things in the outside world: Mr. Zanz's network had been dismantled, the police had put everyone under surveillance, and no one was rising up against the injustice of the realm system. The world was calm again, and the Bradmans were thriving, like parasitical fungus.

However, every night, a silent and secret effervescence reigned on the top floor of the skyscraper. Linus and Toscane gradually dismantled their full-range entertainment units and sneaked the electronic components into Chem's room. He slept only four or five hours a night and had dark rings under his eyes, but his smile every morning was a sign that his work was progressing.

By mid-March an empty carcass was all that was left in

Linus's metal cabinet. Chem announced that his illegal computer was operational: it was as powerful as the ones in the research lab, and it worked online through a cordless system he had managed to code.

"The interference is undetectable," he said with confidence. "Now I have to design the alternate program for the day of the exam. For this, I'll need your help, Cookie."

"My help?" Linus said, surprised. "But I'm no good at programming."

Chem put his index finger on Linus's forehead and smiled. "I need your memory. You're the only person who remembers the exam. I have to use what you know to copy the Great Processor's method."

During the following weeks, Linus and Chem reconstructed the various phases of the exam. As he recounted what he remembered, Linus thought back to the evening in the transit home when he had felt so discouraged that he'd almost swallowed the vanilla tablet. He was truly grateful to Sadko for stopping him.

In fact, he often took advantage of his free time by visiting Mrs. Flavitch, Sadko's mother. He told her about his months spent in the home, the hellish pace of the packaging assembly line, the physical fatigue, the constant surveillance. It always made her cry, but at the same time, the feeling of briefly sharing Sadko's life at a distance seemed to do her good.

When he returned to his room, Linus was exhausted. On reviewing everything that had happened to him since the exam, he realized that he had gone from prison to prison: the transit home, the hotel room in the Eldorado Complex, and now the skyscraper. Only a few stolen moments—when he and Toscane had run down the lawn in the Protected Zone, and his evening at home during Christmas Eve—had provided him with the ephemeral taste of freedom.

He opened the window in his room to let in the outside air. In the evening light, the trees of the Protected Zone loomed in the distance like a wall of greenery. Beyond were his house, his parents, Mieg, Yosh, and his grandmother. Linus could visualize them in every detail. He felt he could almost reach out and touch them, but his fingers met nothing but emptiness.

He was filled with doubt: what if Chem failed?

chapter 27

Two months later, a dense crowd invaded the esplanade in front of the exam center. Entire families, moving in single file, tried to cut through the crowd to get to the main door while others surrounded frightened examinees in tight clusters.

"It's even more disturbing from up here, isn't it?" Chem remarked to Linus. He had just entered Linus's room and joined him by the window.

Linus was completely absorbed as he gazed at the ripples formed by the huge crowd at the foot of the skyscraper.

"If everything works out as planned," Chem whispered, "this will be the last time we witness this kind of gathering. So enjoy it! It's historic!"

Linus looked at him with worry. "Do you think everything will work out?"

Chem nodded. "It has to, Cookie." He took a deep breath. "Everything is all set to go, but there is one complication: I have to be back in my room just before the beginning of the exam. I have to be at the controls to make sure my program is activated at the same time as the Great Processor's."

"Back up here?" Linus shook his head. "That's impossible! Remember the ceremony: we're all supposed to be gathered around Olf Bradman during his speech."

Chem frowned. "It's risky, I know. But I have no choice. If the synchronization isn't perfect, my program won't work. I thought I'd be able to switch it on by remote control, but I wasn't able to set up the remote." He put his large hand on Linus's shoulder. "I'll find the right moment to get away; don't worry. As soon as the ceremony is over, try to come to my room with Toscane."

Linus shut the window. He was nervous. This unforeseen complication seemed insurmountable to him, but there was no time to think about it; the doors of the exam center would be opening very soon. "They're probably waiting for us," he said. "Let's go."

They hurried out of the room. Toscane caught up with them in the hallway. She seemed particularly tense.

"I just realized that my father will be there," she said. "On the podium, next to us. As head of the transit home, he's invited to the opening ceremony of the exam every year." She moaned. "He'll see me! What will I say to him?"

Linus took her hand, but couldn't find words to make her feel better. When they reached the end of the hallway, he pressed the button to call the elevator. Other residents from the top floor were coming out of their rooms. In a few minutes, they would all be grouped around Olf Bradman on the podium overlooking the huge lobby. The examinees would look up to them as representatives of order, the supreme authority, the law, the Great Processor. Their conversion would appear official.

Inside the elevator, Mrs. Flavitch squeezed next to Linus. "I hope the promise you made will come true," she whispered, a bit anxiously.

Linus smiled to cover up his own apprehension. A few days before, he had broken down and told her that she would soon be seeing her son again. It was probably a rash promise, but afterward Mrs. Flavitch had recovered some of her joy. Now she was waiting for the miracle to occur, and Linus was becoming increasingly skeptical that the plan would succeed.

The elevator stopped at the second floor and the door opened onto a semicircular corridor leading to the podium.

"Do you hear that?" Toscane whispered.

Linus and Chem nodded. A buzz of voices reached them from the large lobby. The examinees were already inside the center, waiting for the opening speech. Linus suddenly had stage fright. His legs felt wobbly, so much so that he had to lean on Chem as he walked. When they walked out onto the balcony and got close to the podium, Olf Bradman welcomed them curtly.

"Hurry up!" he snarled. "We're starting!"

Lowering their heads, they went to the side, to stand as far away from Bradman as possible.

"Where's Seth?" Linus asked.

Chem shrugged. Toscane stood next to him, trying to be inconspicuous. Linus noticed the thick, shiny nape of the transit home director's neck a few feet in front of them.

"My father's here," Toscane whispered.

"Don't worry," Linus said reassuringly. "He can't harm us."

She shook her head in despair. "He sees and hears everything. He's worse than a thousand cameras. If he catches sight of us, he won't take his eyes off us."

A silence fell over the lobby, and Olf Bradman's booming voice filled the imposing vaulted hall. "My children," he said warmly, "welcome to the examination center. We all know how important this day is . . ."

Linus wished he could stop up his ears. Not that speech again. It was identical to last year's, when he'd been among the crowd down in the lobby.

". . . you will be leaving the world of childhood and becoming full-fledged citizens," Bradman continued. "In the future, one of you may even have my job."

Linus turned his head slightly. He had spotted Seth below, among the students, puffing his chest out, flushed with pleasure. Clearly he already saw himself in his father's position. Just then, Chem poked Linus gently with his elbow.

"Make sure no one sees me," he mumbled.

Linus shuddered. "Now?"

"Now," Chem said. And he edged away quietly. Treading slowly and cautiously, he retreated to the back of the podium. Linus was terror-stricken. Chem was leaving in the middle of Bradman's speech. Linus didn't dare move,

but his eyes darted from left to right to see if anyone noticed.

"Whatever the outcome, you will have to assume it is
for your own good, the good of your families, and the
good of society as a whole," Bradman continued.

All the managers gathered around him stood facing
the examinees, motionless and dignified, as their posi-
tions required. His brow moist, Linus decided to glance
over his shoulder. Chem had disappeared. It seemed that
no one had noticed.

"Before explaining some of the rules," Bradman said,
"I am indulging a little whim for the opening speech this
year."

Linus turned to face the center of the podium. He was
alarmed: what kind of whim could such an un-whimsical
person possibly indulge?

"I'll let my son introduce this little surprise," Bradman announced. "Seth will join us up here for a minute,
then take his place among you again."

Linus saw Seth cut through the crowd and climb up a
stairway to the podium. When he reached the top of the
stairs, his father handed him the mike. Intrigued, Linus
leaned toward Toscane.

"Do you think he's going to sing?"

Toscane glanced at him with pleading eyes. She was
petrified by her father's presence.

"Last year," Seth began, articulating his words, "certain examinees tried to change the exam scores to suit
their purposes."

Linus gave a start. His heart skipped a beat. What was Seth driving at?

"These examinees thought they could trick the Great Processor. They thought they were so clever. Well, they made a grave error. And to demonstrate this, I'll call on one of them so that you can hear the words of a reformed rebel."

Linus bit his lip and drew blood.

"I call on Linus Hoppe!" Seth announced.

There was a hush. Linus didn't move; he was paralyzed. Seth reiterated his order more vigorously. With a pang in his heart and a dry mouth, Linus walked slowly to the front.

"Good," said Seth, taking him by the shoulders. "I advise you to listen carefully to what this former examinee says. All of you have a great deal to learn from him." He handed Linus the mike and whispered, "Go ahead! Talk to the audience! Tell them what a high opinion you have of our system and the Great Processor. If you slip up, you know the penalty."

In a trancelike state, Linus looked out at the crowd of students. Hundreds of faces were gazing up at him, hundreds of attentive eyes and worried brows. The mike in his hand seemed to weigh a ton. He wished he could raise it to his lips and yell into it what he really thought of the exam. He wished he could shout and tell them to run away and not submit to the torture, to the insane farce that awaited them. He wished he could tell them about his abusive life since the exam. But he couldn't. The threats to his family were real, and Chem was carrying out his plan. For the plan to work, the exam had to take place. So Linus brought the mike to his lips and said in a voice that was almost calm, "I was mistaken. I thought the exam was unfair, but it is fair. Each one of you will realize this within a few hours. You must accept your scores. You must put your destinies into the hands of the Great Processor. He alone can decide what's best for you." Linus reeled. Below, the hundreds of faces were swaying and blurring. The colors blended together and a murmur arose in the assembly. "I thought I could decide for myself what life I wanted. I thought I should fight for my freedom and everyone else's. But I was selfish and conceited." He stopped speaking and looked down at the crowd. He felt as if he were standing at the helm of a ship. His stomach was churning. "If you see me crying," he said in conclusion, as tears rolled down his cheeks, "it's purely from shame."

Seth grabbed the mike from him and shouted, "Yes, given everything he did, Linus Hoppe can certainly be ashamed. And his message is clear: don't even consider imitating him! You'd be making a serious mistake."

Olf Bradman returned to the center of the podium and said solemnly, "And now, proof that there's no favoritism, Seth will go back downstairs and take the exam along with the rest of you. We appeal to you: please be scrupulous in obeying the rules, so that the exam can take place under the best possible conditions."

While a triumphant Seth joined the crowd of

examinees, Linus returned to the back of the podium, head lowered, more humiliated than he had ever been in his life. The ordeal had exhausted him. A commotion of incomprehensible words filled the lobby. He looked around for Toscane, hoping for words of comfort, but couldn't find her. Jostling a few people, he went to the far end of the podium. His friend was nowhere in sight. Suddenly he noticed that the director of the transit home was gone too. His blood froze. The exam was scheduled to start in a few minutes. What if Toscane's father had seen Chem leave? What if he was trying to wreck their plan? Maybe Toscane had followed him to stop him.

With fear in the pit of his stomach, Linus glanced around. A foundation employee was giving out the final instructions, and groups of students were beginning to head for the other floors in the exam center.

Linus knew he had nothing to lose now. Taking advantage of the general confusion, he ran to the elevator. He hoped it wasn't too late.

chapter 28

In the elevator going up, Linus felt more and more frightened. At every landing, he thought he heard voices crying treason. He shook his head. It wasn't possible. His speech had lasted only a few minutes. Even if Toscane's father had followed Chem, he wouldn't have had time to warn everyone.

By the time Linus reached the thirtieth floor, his hands were trembling. The long corridor was silent, and as he rounded the curve, the corridor seemed to get narrower. He was feeling dizzy again. He leaned against the wall to catch his breath and pricked up his ears. Nothing. Not the slightest whisper or sign of life. He hugged the wall until he reached Chem's door. It was shut.

His heart beating faster, Linus put his ear against the door. Silence. He put his trembling hand on the doorknob. The door clicked open. Linus was so surprised, he almost let out a cry.

The May sunshine streamed into the room through the open windows. He could even hear the birds singing. Chem should have been there, hunched over his computer, ready to activate his program. But there was no one. With great apprehension, Linus entered the room and went to the metal cabinet where the homemade machine was hidden. He kneeled down and opened it.

The illegal computer was there, where it belonged.

What did that mean? The engine was humming; it seemed to be on sleep. Just as he was about to put his hand on the touch screen, Linus heard a muffled noise coming from behind him. He turned. No one. He dashed out of the room and glanced up and down the corridor. It was deserted. He heard the noise again. It sounded like a distant voice, a plaintive cry.

"The bathroom," Linus mumbled.

He went to the far end of the room and tried to open the door. He couldn't: the lock was jammed. Then he distinctly heard someone calling from inside.

"Chem?" he called softly.

He heard a groan in response.

"Is that you?" Linus asked.

"Hmmm . . ."

Linus jiggled the doorknob. It was no use. Someone had locked the door and taken the key, leaving Chem gagged in the bathroom. "I'll try to get you out," Linus said.

"Hmmm-*hmmm*," the voice answered.

Linus's mind raced. Since all the rooms were identical, there was a chance that the locks were identical too. All he had to do was get his own key. "I'll be right back!" he said, dashing into the corridor.

He had barely stepped out of the room when he heard the elevator doors opening and people shouting. Panic-stricken, Linus froze, unsure what to do. The voices came closer. He thought he recognized Bradman's voice. There was no time to hesitate; in a flash, he darted back into Chem's room and closed the door behind him. He had to find some way of jamming it.

Linus glanced around in a panic. The bed! He started to drag the bed to the door. It wasn't easy sliding the legs across the thick carpeting. Braced against the bed, his muscles tense, Linus heard Chem's voice, quite distinctly, coming from the bathroom.

"Linus! We're here!"

Meanwhile, the noises in the corridor were growing louder. Bradman was approaching. Linus felt his strength increase tenfold from an outflow of adrenaline. He dragged the bed all the way to the door as a barricade.

Chem called out to him from the bathroom. "Linus, are you there? I'm with Toscane! We're locked in!"

Linus ran to the bathroom. "I'm here," he said through the door. "Wait one second!"

He ran to the bed, made sure that he had pushed it flat against the door, and looked around for other heavy objects to put on top of it. The beverage machine wouldn't budge, but he was able to move the metal pedestal table. Red and sweaty, he lifted it and dumped it on top of the bed. Just as he was wedging the heavy tabletop against the door, he saw the doorknob move.

He paled when he heard someone say, "I don't understand, Mr. Bradman. I left it unlocked a few minutes ago."

It was Toscane's father's voice. Linus reconstructed in

his mind the probable sequence of events. The director of the transit home had followed Chem to the top floor, and Toscane had run after him. When they reached Chem's room, the director succeeded in overpowering Chem, then Toscane. He must have dragged them into the bathroom, gagged them with towels, tied their hands behind their backs, locked the door, and gone downstairs to warn Bradman.

"Break down this door!" Bradman ordered angrily.

Terrified, Linus watched the panel move as the director began to pummel the door with his shoulder. Fortunately, the bed and the table were an adequate barricade—at least for the time being.

"Linus!" Chem yelled hoarsely from the bathroom.

Linus rushed to the bathroom door. "I'm listening!"

"Our arms are attached to the legs of the sink! I managed to get rid of my gag, but that's all I can do!"

"The exam is about to start!" Linus said in a panic, glancing worriedly at the door, which was shaking more than before.

"Listen to me carefully," Chem said. "You'll have to activate the program. I'll tell you what to do."

Linus shut his eyes. The banging on the door intensified. Shouts echoed in the corridor. Bradman would surely get reinforcements, and then it would be too late to sabotage the exam.

"Tell me what to do!" Linus cried out.

"First move the computer next to this door. Hurry up!"

Linus dashed to the metal cabinet and dragged the computer over to the bathroom. "Done!" he said.

"Now touch the left side of the screen."

Linus obeyed. The screen lit up immediately.

"What do you see?" Chem asked.

"Numbers!" Linus replied. "0:00:45!"

"It's the countdown!" Chem groaned. "You have forty-five seconds."

The banging had stopped and Linus doubted that the silence was a good sign.

"Do you see that round dial under the screen, on the right?" Chem asked.

"Yes!"

"Turn the dial all the way!"

Linus seized the dial and turned it. "More numbers! They look like frequency measurements!"

"That's normal," Chem said. "Is the diode above lit up?"

"Yes, it's flashing!"

"You're doing well," Chem said encouragingly. "Now, in a clear, intelligible voice, you're going to enter the code I'm about to give you. The vocal transcriber will give you access to the Great Processor's memory. Are you ready?"

"Yes."

"The code is Inv-slash-Tot-slash-Ex-slash-Cookie."

Cookie! Linus smiled. Chem had a knack for making jokes in the worst situations. He took a deep breath and was about to repeat the code when the door was hit so violently that the hinges cracked. He cried out.

"What happened?" Chem asked.

"They're breaking down the door!" Linus said in a panic.

"The code!" Chem yelled.

Linus looked at the screen in despair. The number was getting smaller. Only eleven seconds left. He made an enormous effort to concentrate and repeated the code slowly and clearly.

As soon as he had finished, the diode turned red.

"That's normal!" Chem said. "Now, reach down on the right side of the computer! You'll find two cables: plug them simultaneously into the two sockets located under the screen."

Linus groped and caught the cables. He plugged them into the sockets feverishly.

"Look at the screen!" Chem ordered.

"I see two graphs!"

"Describe them."

"One is ascending and the other is descending. They're going to intersect! That's it! They're intersecting!"

"And now what?"

"There's a message being displayed! Inv-slash-Tot-slash-Ex-slash-Eff-slash-Cookie."

Silence. Linus stared at the screen, hypnotized, unsure whether the message was a good sign. His concentration was so intense that he no longer heard the door being struck or the people yelling in the corridor. After a long pause, he shuddered. Slowly, he leaned his forehead against the door of the bathroom. "Chem? Are you there? What should I do now?"

"Nothing, Cookie," Chem answered. "You've done it!"

Linus stared at the bathroom door as if it had spoken, and he smiled at it with a silly expression. "So that's it," he mumbled. "The Great Processor will go completely crazy." All his pent-up tension was released. In a choking voice, he called out, "Toscane! Can you hear me?"

"Hmmm!"

"She can't speak," Chem explained. "She's still gagged. But I see tears in her eyes, Cookie. I think that's her way of saying thank you."

Linus straightened his back slowly. He felt disoriented. Looking down, he saw that the illegal computer had put itself on sleep. It had evidently downloaded its program into the Great Processor, and now, even if it was switched off, it was too late to stop the process. Linus turned to the door. The bed and the pedestal table had been displaced by a few millimeters. Suddenly he realized there was no noise in the corridor. He listened carefully. There were no voices and no one was trying to break into the room. "What's going to happen now?" Linus asked Chem.

"The Great Processor must have already sent out a warning signal," Chem explained. "The monitoring staff will soon realize that something's drastically wrong." He started laughing, the sound echoing in the bathroom. "They won't be able to do anything," he added. "In a few minutes, the exam will be over and that will be it for the Bradmans!"

Alone in the room, Linus smiled wearily. Someone had

probably come to tell Bradman that there was a big problem and that was why he had stopped trying to break down the door. The emergency was elsewhere.

Linus walked over to the open window. It was a beautiful day. A flawless blue sky was spread out over the city as far as the eye could see.

"How about trying to get us out of here?" Chem called out from the bathroom.

Linus turned, his face serene.

"Get you out of there? What for? Don't you like fancy bathrooms anymore?"

"Very funny, Cookie!"

epilogue

"Is everyone comfortable?" Yosh asked. "Can I go on?"

He looked at the people crowded inside his parents' apartment. Mr. and Mrs. Hoppe were there, along with Chem's parents, Mrs. Flavitch, Linus's grandmother, and his own parents. Sitting on the floor, around the coffee table, on which Yosh's mother had placed refreshments and cake, were Linus, Chem, Mieg, Toscane, and Sadko. Everyone signaled to show they were ready.

"Let's start," Yosh announced, pressing the button on the remote control.

The antique DVD player switched on, and the first shots appeared on the screen. Yosh's father had recorded the disc on the night of the exam. It consisted of three hours of news reports on the events following the disclosure of the results.

The anchorwoman was presenting a direct report from the exam center. A huge crowd could be seen milling in front of the door. The atmosphere was tense; people were screaming and shoving one another. Suddenly the image flickered, blurred, and froze.

"Oh, no!" Yosh moaned. "What happened?"

"It's an old player," his mother said apologetically. "It's temperamental. Give it a little shove, Yosh."

Yosh got up and tapped the set, and the player started up again. The special correspondent explained that parents had been demonstrating in front of the exam center for two hours and that some of them were trying to get inside the building. The police had been rushed to the scene. Two men grabbed the reporter's mike and spoke into the camera.

"What's happening is unacceptable!" one of the men shouted. "I'm a lawyer in the Higher Court. The members of my family have been brilliant Realm One citizens for two generations. My daughter is an excellent student and she's just been relegated to Realm Two. It's an outrage! A hoax!"

Then the other man cut in and began to yell. "All Realm One parents are in the same situation as this gentleman. Our children are the victims of a colossal mistake. We can't accept these scores."

The crowd carried him a short distance away while a disheveled woman appeared before the camera.

"Give us back our children!" she shouted hoarsely. "I've just learned that my two sons have been sent to Realm Three! They've done nothing wrong! They aren't rebels or delinquents! I won't leave until we find out the truth: the exam was rigged!"

Other tearful or outraged parents streamed in front of the camera. Whether from Realm Two or Realm One, they were all protesting for the same reason and making identical demands: they denounced the Great Processor and wanted their children returned. Several parents even became the self-appointed spokesmen of Realm Three or Realm Four parents who couldn't be present.

"We're speaking on their behalf!" proclaimed an elegant white-haired woman. "If they were allowed to leave their zones, they too would show their anger, just like all of us! They have a right to know what happened! We're all equal in the face of this outrage!"

Eyes riveted to the screen, Chem shook his head. "When I think it had to come to this for them to realize that people in Realm Three and Four aren't monsters . . ."

"Shhh!" Mieg said. "We can't hear."

The reporter on screen had recovered his mike. His face was red and his eyes shone feverishly.

"What's happening here is incredible!" he said. "It's been decades since we've had such social unrest. The entire population is up in arms against the managers of the exam center, who've retreated to the upper stories of this skyscraper. The police are unable to cope. According to our sources, not a single examinee has been allowed to leave the building yet."

The cameraman zoomed in on the upper stories of the building. Hands could be seen waving from an open window.

"That's us!" Toscane cried out, jumping to her feet. "Look!"

Three laughing faces could be seen in the distance: Chem's, Linus's, and Toscane's.

"That's when we recognized you," Grandma said. "We were watching the news broadcast. We'd been looking for you for such a long time!"

"So had we," Chem's mother said. "When we recognized Chem's face, it was an incredible shock!"

"And that's when your father made his decision, Linus," Mrs. Hoppe added. "I'd never seen him so excited!"

"Shhh! We'll get to that later," Mr. Hoppe said.

The camera continued to focus on the faces on the thirtieth floor of the building.

"When I saw the police arrive on the esplanade, I knew we had succeeded!" Linus said, his cheeks flushed.

"Linus broke down the bathroom door by hitting it with the metal table," Toscane said. "It was unbelievable!"

Chem laughed. "Fortunately it was a shoddy door or we would still be there."

"And thank goodness Linus had his little brainstorm," Toscane added. "There! Look! I think you can see us throwing papers out the window."

The camera panned to sheets of paper fluttering down from the top floor and landing on the angry crowd. The reporter elbowed his way through the sea of bodies, looking for someone who had picked one up.

"What's it all about?" he asked a man in overalls, who was brandishing a sheet.

"It's one of the kids up there," the man replied, pointing at the building. "He's just thrown this down. It has writing on it."

"Sir, would you mind reading what it says in front of the camera?"

The man cleared his throat and started reading in an emotional voice. "Your children have just been through a dreadful ordeal. They are presently in recovery rooms, where they will be given a drug that will erase their memories. They'll forget what they've been through. Don't desert them! Go rescue them!"

There was a murmur in the living room.

"Did you write that, Linus?" Sadko asked.

"Yes," Linus replied modestly. "I knew that this time people would believe me. If I had told them the truth about the exam when no one was questioning it, they wouldn't have listened. But now they were all concerned."

Onscreen, other people were parading in front of the camera, holding sheets of paper and saying the same thing. Their anger was growing. Suddenly the report was interrupted and the studio anchorwoman came back on the air.

"Now comes your hour of glory, Dad!" Mieg said proudly.

Mr. Hoppe blushed and propped his chin in his hands while Toscane nibbled on some cake and Sadko poured himself another glass of fruit juice.

"We have been told that a prominent member of the Economic Observatory, Mr. Tobias Hoppe, is presently in our studio," the anchorwoman announced. "He has disclosures to make concerning the managers of the exam center. Under the circumstances, we feel we should hear what he has to say."

Mr. Hoppe was in the studio. In the background, Mieg's and Yosh's silhouettes flitted across a curtain. Mr. Hoppe sat down facing the anchorwoman.

"You didn't even take the time to put on a necktie?" Linus said with surprise.

Everyone in the living room laughed, then fell silent. Onscreen, Mr. Hoppe was unfolding a printout.

"My department has been investigating the financial transactions of the Bradman group for several months," he began. "We found that a portion of his profits from his various suburban shopping centers is being used to subsidize a foundation directed by Mr. Bradman's adopted son, Seth."

"Is this foundation in any way connected to the exam center?" the anchorwoman asked.

"It is," Mr. Hoppe replied. "Last year, acting illegally, the foundation purchased the exam center's offices and took over the institution. Prior to that, Mr. Olf Bradman was already one of the managing officers, but this purchase gave him more power. The foundation bought the silence of the people who were actively opposed to the Great Processor's abuses. Today, these abuses are plain for everyone to see." Mr. Hoppe waved his sheet of paper. "The figures are here! They come straight from the Economic Observatory. They show that the Bradmans, father and son, are guilty of tax evasion, corruption, and monopoly. These are very serious charges! The future of our children is at stake! We can't possibly allow such individuals to control their fates." Mr. Hoppe's voice broke from emotion. "I'm well positioned to say so because my son, Linus, is presently being held captive in the exam center building. I thought he was dead. And for his sake, I'm going to join the parents' demonstration." Mr. Hoppe stood up, looking dignified, and left the studio.

"You were good," Mrs. Hoppe said. "Very good."

"And very moving," Grandma added.

"The important thing was that my speech made the minister of education join the movement," Mr. Hoppe said modestly.

"And other ministers followed suit," Chem's father pointed out. "They had no choice! They would have discredited themselves if they had supported Bradman."

"Yes, they saw trouble brewing!" Chem laughed. "It was the perfect tactic!"

Sadko put down his glass. "Things were so crazy that the rumor even reached us in the transit home," he said. "And since the director was being held in the skyscraper, we all left the STZ. It was a real uprising! If your father had seen it, Toscane . . ."

"He'd have had a stroke!" Toscane sighed. "But for the moment, he's in a rest home. You can bet it's the first occasion he's ever spent so much time in bed."

"By the way, have you decided what you'd like to do?" Mrs. Hoppe asked her.

Toscane turned to her. "If you don't mind, I'd love to move in with you for a while."

Linus smiled at his parents and blushed slightly when he met Toscane's gaze. Meanwhile, Yosh pressed the fast-forward button on the remote control. The same anchorwoman appeared onscreen later in the evening, her features drawn.

"We are going live to the exam center, where the doors are being opened and the managers are being arrested. This year's exam has been declared null and void by the Ministry of Education. In fact, our entire system of social ranking has been called into question."

Yosh fast-forwarded again. The last shots showed several foundation managers, including Seth and Olf Bradman, walking through the crowd, flanked by policemen. Parents and children, reunited at last, formed a hostile row of onlookers. It was evening, but Seth's features could be seen under the floodlights. Yosh froze the frame.

Everyone in the living room was motionless and silent. Yosh's parents, clearly distressed, could barely look at the screen.

Yosh went up close to it and said faintly, "That's my brother. He looks like me, but at the same time . . . he isn't like me at all. We were born of the same parents, but in the end, that's not what really matters. What matters is one's upbringing." Then he turned his moonlike face toward Linus and Chem. "The other thing that matters are the friends we make." Then he pointed the remote control at the screen and turned the set off.

After a pause, Mrs. Flavitch got up, shaken. She

looked at each person, held out her arms, and opened her palms. There were two permanent scars on her skin.

Linus lowered his eyes and looked at his own hands. He ran a finger over his own scars. On the night of the exam, Dr. Ambrose had operated on all of them, one after the other, far into the night, to remove all the implants.

"Let these marks be a reminder of what we've been through," Mrs. Flavitch said. "I want to thank all of you for what you did."

● ● ●

Later—while the adults were enjoying drinks brought by Mr. and Mrs. Hoppe—Linus, Chem, Yosh, Sadko, and Toscane slipped away and went up to the seventh floor of Yosh's building, to Mr. Zanz's former apartment. It had been unoccupied for a year. The door, forced open by the police, had remained ajar. They went in silently, with heavy hearts, as though in a sanctuary.

Linus lingered in the hallway, looking at the rows of books that had remained unopened for a long time. He ran his hand over the worn spines nostalgically. When he joined the others in the small dusty living room, Toscane put her arms around his shoulders and held him tightly.

"Now that I'm living here again," Yosh said softly, "I'll do something about Mr. Zanz's possessions." He turned to Linus. "You should take his books. I think he would have been pleased to give them to you."

Linus nodded. Chem kneeled down to pick up a small

case that had fallen from the table. He opened it. Inside he found a pair of eyeglasses. He closed the case carefully.

"I think he would have been proud of us," Yosh continued. "It was his life's dream to see the downfall of the Great Processor."

"There's no doubt about that," Chem said, his eyes moist. "He would have said to us, 'So, children, what are your plans now?' "

They drew close to one another in silent agreement. The only thing they knew for sure was that they would be able to stay together, regardless of their original realms. Everything else had yet to be invented.

Linus smiled despite his sadness. "You're right, Mr. Zanz," he said, looking around at the empty apartment. "Our future is ours to create."

ABOUT THE AUTHOR

Anne-Laure Bondoux was born near Paris in 1971. She has written several novels for young people in varied genres and has received numerous literary prizes in her native France.